NORTHERN ESCAPE

CINDY FOLK

SPLASH
PUBLISHING

© 2021 Cindy Folk

Northern Escape: Ripple Effect Trilogy
First edition, June 2021

Splash Publishing
Saskatoon, Saskatchewan

cindyfolkauthor.com

Editing: Shayla Raquel, shaylaraquel.com
Cover Design: Monica Haynes, thethatchery.com
Interior Formatting: Melinda Martin, melindamartin.me

ISBN: 978-1-7775231-0-7 (print)

To everyone who believed I could.

CONTENTS

PROLOGUE

THERE WERE TEN IN THE TEN-PASSENGER VAN. IT WAS snug, but she didn't mind. Where they were headed, Grace wouldn't have to worry about food or lodging—someone else was taking care of that, someone else was in charge. It felt so good to be able to just close her eyes, blend in and be.

Her head bumped against the window in time with the tires hitting the potholes in the road. Unable to sleep, Grace listened with her eyes still closed. Her seat mate hummed to herself as she flipped through a magazine. The couple in front of her was talking about whether they'd remembered to turn off the water and lock the front door. They planned on making a phone call at the lodge.

In the back seat, the wiry guy with the tattoos was strumming on his guitar. It wasn't a song that Grace recognized, and the repetition led her to believe he was monkeying around with a new song of his own. Not bad and surprisingly not annoying given the close quarters.

Grace tried to ignore the man sitting two to her right. He probably didn't remember her anyway. It was years ago and so much had happened since then. Even so, she wondered where her life might be had she made a different choice that night.

She knew he was not what she needed right now, either. What she needed was *anything* but that.

The man driving seemed to be the very essence of the North. He was quiet and calm and appeared fully capable of taking this group of city dwellers to the bush for six days. Six days! Would that be enough? Would she know what to do when this week—not even a week—was over? Where would she go so she couldn't be found? Grace had no idea. She would have to get in touch with her dad—but how, without exposing herself or putting him in harm's way?

Money. That was another issue. She needed a job—that paid in cash—and a place to stay. Survival was the key right now.

Rattled, Grace took long, slow breaths.

He doesn't know where she is. How could he? This was such a last-minute decision.

CHAPTER 1

I Wished to Live Deliberately

—Henry David Thoreau

"DO YOU HAVE ANY ROOMS AVAILABLE?" GRACE ASKED the dark-skinned woman behind the counter who studied her before looking down at the computer screen. Grace knew she should have changed before checking in. Her wavy, dark brown hair was pulled through the back of her cap into a low ponytail. She always wore it that way and cursed herself for being so stupid. He would be able to track her more easily if she didn't change her appearance soon.

"Yes, we have two open on the third floor. Would you like the Orchid Room or the Tulip?" she asked.

"The Tulip," Grace answered in a low voice, trying not to make eye contact, wishing she had covered her gray eyes with sunglasses. Accepting the room key, she grabbed her pack and headed up the stairs to the left of the counter.

Pulling her cap off, Grace gave her hair a shake as she climbed, remembering . . .

"Where are you going?" he had demanded.

"To get groceries," she'd replied.

Appalled, he asked, "Looking like that?"

Grace looked down at her outfit. She was wearing jeans and a T-shirt.

"What's wrong with how I look?" She knew the backtalk would tick him off, but she didn't care.

"Put your hair up and wear this." He threw a sweatshirt at her.

Grace caught the sweatshirt and walked to the door without putting it on.

He'd been getting pushier and pushier, and Grace was tired of it. She pulled the door open and began to step through it when a hand reached over her shoulder. As he pushed the door shut, it glanced off Grace's shoulder before cutting into the side of her lower leg.

She cried out and fell to the floor.

Yanking Grace away from the door, he slammed it shut and slid the chain in place.

"Shut up. You want everyone hearing?"

"Maybe I do!" Grace yelled back at him.

He lunged at her, and she welcomed a slap to her face. At least then she would have evidence of the terrible abuses he inflicted on her daily, most of which left no mark. He was a sociopath who controlled her every move and was smart enough not to leave evidence of his mistreatment. Instead, his face turned cold and he grabbed the purse out of Grace's hand.

"We'll order in," he stated and walked to the kitchen to make the call for delivery.

Finding the third-floor Tulip room, Grace slid her key in and clicked open the lock. Stepping into the dark room, curtains drawn, she didn't bother to turn on the light. Shutting the door behind her, Grace leaned on it and slowly slid to the floor just as the silent tears began to trail down her face.

Blinking through the blurriness, her eyes focused on something pink. A flower, a tulip. Pulling her T-shirt up to dry her face, Grace saw why the room was called the Tulip Room. It was pretty—the carpet, the wallpaper, the curtains.

Standing, Grace walked to the bedside table and turned on the lamp. She picked up her bag from the floor and pulled out what she'd been able to bring along. A few clothes, toiletries, driver's license, cell phone, and a big envelope of cash. She'd emptied out her account the day before, knowing she wouldn't be able to access it without him knowing where she was.

Grace had gone to the bank in the early afternoon—he'd been sleeping, still recovering from his previous shift—praying he wouldn't wake while she was gone. She had put some food in the Crock-Pot and started a few meal preparations to make it look as if she had been at it for a while. She had let him sleep a bit longer than normal just so he would have to eat quickly and run out the door. He regularly checked the account, and she had to be sure he didn't look at it again before heading out to work for the night.

"Why did you go to Walmart?"

"To get some personal items."

He had set his fork down, then sat up straight. "Like what?"

"Lotion, toothpaste, deodorant, that kind of stuff." Grace had shrugged, hoping he'd be satisfied.

Nodding, he reached for his glass and took a sip of water.

Maybe she had actually convinced him.

But then: "Be specific."

Her cheeks flushed. "Elastics for my hair, Tylenol, pads, and tampons." She no longer had the energy to make things up, and what was the point? He'd be tallying up the cost in his head, figuring out whether what she was reporting was plausible.

"I'm not made of money, you know," he said, eyes narrowed.

Grace lowered her voice, and tears welled up in her eyes. "These are necessities."

"It's more than I buy myself," he countered.

She pinched her lips together.

"You have a problem with that?"

"No." Saying that she was capable and willing to work wouldn't help anything. She swallowed her resentment, excused herself, and started on the dishes.

Grace had learned her lesson a few months earlier when, beyond frustrated, she broke her own hand punching the bedroom wall. He'd just walked out, heard the bang, and marched back in, furious that she might have damaged the apartment. His eyes had softened when he saw her hand sitting at an odd angle. He gently walked Grace to the car and rushed her to the emergency room.

Flashing his badge at the hospital, he'd bypassed the lines and had her X-rayed and casted up in no time, saying that she'd tripped carrying her bike up the stairs after a ride. The story was believable and, since no one had asked her what had happened, his sweet looks and actions ensured Grace was given the best care before she was sent home.

This was the man Grace had fallen in love with. The take-charge hero who ensured she had everything she needed. He had a very soft, sensitive side, as long as everything was going his way. However, easily set off, he took the demands of his career in police enforcement out on Grace.

And so, although things were good between them for a while, it was on the ride home from the hospital that Grace began planning her escape. Knowing any online research would be traceable, she took steps to carefully put her plan in place. A walk was designed to go by the bus depot to discreetly grab a pamphlet on bus routes, schedules, and prices. A trip to the library allowed the opportunity to look at maps of Ottawa and figure out a place to stay.

Looking around her room, she realized that she'd lucked out with this bed and breakfast. It was lovely. Her stomach grumbled, and Grace realized she hadn't eaten all day. Knowing there was an Irish pub a few blocks away, she freshened up and changed into a button-up plaid shirt—a shirt she'd bought a couple of years back, but one that he had never liked.

As she walked down the tree-lined street on that early June evening, Grace decided it was the perfect shirt to wear in order to stay under the radar. If he sent word to his buddies on the police force here, he would be describing a girl who lived almost exclusively in T-shirts, sweatshirts, and jeans.

She was aware of the grenade in her backpack. She had considered tossing her phone altogether, knowing she could easily be tracked if she were to use it, but she couldn't bring herself to, as it could be a lifeline just as easily as her undoing. She had removed the SIM card so that it couldn't be traced. Given that without it, she could no longer make calls, send text messages, or connect to the internet, its only function now was as a camera.

Stepping into the pub, Grace was taken back to happier times during college when she had often come there with friends. She found her favorite table in the back corner and admired the quiet elegance of the room until the waitress came to take her order. Since she couldn't look up anything on her phone, she read the entertainment chalkboard hanging on the wall while she waited for her fish and chips. Sipping her beer, she allowed herself to hope that the worst was behind her. She'd done it, and her freedom was worth the challenges of finding work or a place to live. The death he'd promised her should Grace leave him wasn't even enough to worry her at the moment. Death was more welcome than the hell she'd been living, essentially held captive in her own home.

As the waitress delivered her meal, she raised an eyebrow and said with an Irish lilt, "You look like the cat that ate the canary."

Grace just smiled and reached for the ketchup, not even questioning why thoughts of death should make her so happy.

CHAPTER 2

Things Do Not Change; We Change

—Henry David Thoreau

G RACE TIPTOED DOWN THE HALL TO THE THIRD-FLOOR bathroom. It was early, and the house was quiet. She didn't want to wake any of the other guests at the bed and breakfast, but the squeaky turn of her doorknob and the creak of the floorboards as she walked announced her presence.

"Shhh . . ." she wanted to whisper. "Don't tell them I'm here."

Giving up on her stealth moves, she shut the bathroom door with a groan and a clunk and slid the lock into place. Splashing water on her face, she looked in the mirror and was not surprised to see her mother looking back. Grace saw her every morning, and today her puffy eyes gave her sadness away. Her mother had had the same gray eyes and wavy, dark brown hair, but she'd gotten her long limbs from her father. Drying her face, Grace pushed the towel against her eyes to stop the sting of tears that had started yet again.

I need you so much, Mom, she thought. *This never would have happened if you were still here. You would have seen what was happening, and your momma bear temper would have sent him running.*

Bullies by nature don't want to be challenged, and Grace wouldn't have been worth the effort. Instead, charming and chiseled, he had seen her weaknesses and had taken advantage of them. Dad was too grief-stricken to notice. He had completely focused on his new life in order to keep the pain locked away. Seeing his daughter only made it harder for him. He, too, saw his wife every time he looked at Grace, and it brought back the loss over and over. Good or bad, Grace saw her mother every time she looked in the mirror.

She loitered in the lobby of the bed and breakfast on Laurier Street until the Jamaican woman who had checked her in the evening before welcomed her into the dining room with a big, beautiful smile. The table was big enough for eight, likely the number of guests that could stay in the home. She was relieved to have her choice of seat.

Grace had let everything out last night. She'd shed tears of fear, loss, grief, and panic. It was a release of all the feelings that had been pent up and not acknowledged for . . . how long? A year? Two? Certainly, the last year had been bad. Horrible. But the last six months had been the worst.

He had allowed Grace to mourn her mother before showing the full extent of his ability to manipulate and control. He knew Grace's dad was distracted with his new life, his soon-to-be new wife, and her sweet little children. They were adorable, and good on him for being willing to go through all that again. But Grace wasn't ready. *How could he be?* She already knew the answer even if she didn't like it. Mom had been sick for so long, and she had made him promise to move on.

And so, she had moved in with *him*. She decided not to think his name. This was a new start, and it would be a way to keep him and his control in the past. Grace studied her right hand. It wasn't pretty like her left one anymore. It wasn't bad, but it was damaged, misshapen. Not bad enough for others to notice, but she saw the difference and felt the throbbing ache, a reminder of the frustration and fear that she had tried to rid herself of. Grace wondered if that pain would always remain a part of her—just like the abuse she had suffered would always be imprinted on her soul.

She gratefully received her breakfast of bacon, eggs, rye toast, butter and marmalade preserves, grapefruit, orange juice, and, thank the Lord, strong and steaming hot coffee. It felt wonderful to have someone take care of her in this sunny, warm room. Wallpaper with bright, happy flowers covered the walls. A little gaudy, perhaps, but it fit well with the old furniture. Grace felt like she was in England about to have tea with the queen. She found herself dreaming that she was safely hidden away in another country far, far away from him.

If only that could happen. Grace knew it could never be. *He* would know if she left the country. Over the months, years, he'd shown her that he had the ability to track people. One morning, he had come home rumpled and tired after a night shift and told Grace, who had just woken up and was making coffee, that so-and-so had left for Mexico that morning at six. She'd asked if he'd bumped into them, and he'd answered, "No, I just keep tabs on people I want to keep tabs on. I've got access to systems that are better than Facebook," he'd said with a sneer. They had argued about whether she should get a Facebook account just before he'd left for work the night before. "Facebook only tells you what people want you to know. You know, happy things."

Right. She got it. She wouldn't be advertising, "My boyfriend is emotionally abusive and threatens to kill me if I leave. Often. He makes me dress a certain way and has made me quit my job, twice, because he didn't like the men at the office. They were either too young or too good-look- ing. He also makes me go to an all-women's gym and, even then, ensures I dress appropriately. And if I leave, he'll be able to track me, even if I don't post where I am going on Facebook." That would be her *last* post.

And so, as Grace ate, still not sure where she was going next or what she was going to do when she got there, she flipped through the pamphlets she'd picked up in the lobby. She knew she couldn't stay in Ottawa—it was too obvious. It was a major center, and her hometown.

It was the first place her psycho ex-boyfriend would look. She could easily be spotted as she made her way around downtown. Although a major center, it wasn't a big city and, unless you lived in the suburbs, it would be hard to hide out. The suburbs had zero appeal, though. She might as well be dead if she had to live there. Living in the suburbs would just make her feel lonelier. People in the suburbs had families. She had lost hers and wasn't sure if she would ever trust anyone enough to have a family of her own.

Thank God they hadn't gotten pregnant. Grace would have been forever tied to him and his cruelty. She hated to think how he would have poisoned her relationship with her kids. He was a master manipulator, and if he was kind to the kids, a big *if*, he would make her look weak and undermine her at every step. Grace was sure it would've been heartbreaking . . . or would've ended very badly.

Why, why had I jumped into the relationship so quickly? she chastised herself for the thousandth time. He had wormed his way in while she was worrying about her mom. He had been there to drive her home from the hospital after dark. He was handsome and had been sweet and, for goodness sakes, he was a police officer—he would protect her.

Grace's friends did not trust him. They, too, were charmed by him in the beginning, but soon their warmness faded and they saw through the façade. They turned wary. She had tried to reassure them by defending his actions: "He just loves me so much." And: "He isn't really as confident as he appears." Eventually, it was only herself she made excuses to: "Maybe if I am just more agreeable, he will loosen up and trust me." In the end, Grace just put on a brave face and pretended everything was fine.

Coming back to reality, she took another bite of toast and said thank you as her coffee was refilled. Another girl had come to the table and looked preoccupied and ready for work. She was in a rush, and that suited Grace just fine. The fewer people she spoke to, the better.

Grace put the pamphlet of the art museum to the back of the pile. She would love to go and wander for hours and let her soul go to the places that art took her, but it would be too dangerous, too public. She wanted to check out the rowing club as well. It would be a dream to row on the beautiful Ottawa River again. She had moved to Peterborough after college to work, and it was there that she'd fallen in love with rowing and the regattas that took her to various towns and cities. She missed the close-knit community of her rowing club and the lifestyle she'd enjoyed before she met him. Before everything changed.

Sipping her coffee, Grace thought again about the club here. She would love to hang out with friends again. Having hidden her secrets for so long, she hadn't had a lot of heart-to-heart talks in a while. For a moment, Grace allowed herself the luxury of imagining a friend with whom she could exchange harmless secrets and dreams. It had been too long. But no, the rowing club would be one of the first places he would look for her.

And so, she flipped to the next pamphlet, looking for ideas.

This one read:

Northern Adventure Tours — Come north and get back to nature! Fishing trips or artistic retreats. Our trips are five days and five nights long. They include food, lodging, and transportation to and from the

*Dumais Lodge on the beautiful Thompson Lake. You
will have access to our canoes and boats while here.
The itinerary is as follows . . .*

Her heart beat faster. This was perfect; she could disappear for a few days and get her head on straight. She could pay with the cash in her backpack so there would be no chance of her whereabouts being traced. She would be safe.

But when does it start? What day is it today? Tuesday. Grace looked at the pamphlet. There was an artists' retreat starting today. The bus would leave at 1:00 P.M. from The Lieutenant's Pump pub on Elgin Street. She knew where that was and could easily walk from here. Grace asked to use the phone in the front office and held her breath that there might still be room.

The phone rang four, five times. *Please pick up, please pick up . . .*

"Northern Adventure Tours. Cody speaking."

"Yes, hello. I was wondering about the excursion you have leaving today. The artists' retreat. There wouldn't by any chance be room for one more, would there?"

"Actually, yes, you're in luck. We had a cancellation just this morning, so you would be doing me a huge favor. Can you be at The Lieutenant's Pump at twelve thirty? You know where it is?"

"I can. I sure do. That's great, see you then!"

"Your name?"

"Oh, right." She hesitated. Should she give him her real name? She wanted to be her real self again and didn't want to lose her name on top of all the other parts that had been chipped away over the months and years.

"Grace. Grace Rhodes." Her maternal grandmother's maiden name. She had always loved the name and didn't think *he* would know for sure that it was his Grace.

His Grace. Her stomach lurched.

"Okay, great. Glad you can make it," Cody answered, pausing as he wrote her name down. "So, this trip is for artists of any kind. We combine canoeing and hiking with time for yourself at various locations. It allows you the opportunity to do what you love, whether it be painting, sketching, writing, poetry, photography, or whatever you like. You don't need to be an expert and, you know, it is so beautiful up there that even if you aren't an artist when you arrive, you'll leave with the eyes of someone who appreciates the beauty of it all at the end. It is inevitable."

"Awesome. That sounds wonderful." Grace searched for something else to say. "I like to take pictures and write."

"Perfect. Sounds like you'll fit right in. We have people of all ages coming. Pack some long pants, shorts, T-shirts, and a sweatshirt. If you have a rain jacket, that will come in handy for keeping dry. Basically, we have everything else you need. Oh, and don't forget your toothbrush. That'd be gross."

Chuckling, Grace said, "Thanks for the reminder. Okay, I'll see you just after lunch."

And with that, she had a plan. At least for the next few days.

CHAPTER 3

What Lies Ahead

—Henry David Thoreau

GLANCING AT HER WATCH, GRACE SAW IT WAS ALREADY after nine. She packed her bags, paid for the night's lodging, and headed out the front door with a rowing cap pulled low on her face, unwilling to part with the security it gave her. Grace was traveling light with just her backpack and enough clothing for a few days. She would wash her clothes in the lake if necessary.

The artists' retreat was appealing, being that she was a bit of a shutterbug with an untapped creative side. Grace would actually be pretty pumped about this little adventure if it weren't for the knot in her stomach and the tension in her neck. That being said, it was the perfect escape. In her pack was a notebook that could be used as part of her cover. It would give her an opportunity to get away from the crowd and get the troubling thoughts out of her head and onto paper. Her journal had helped her survive the past two years, and she knew it wouldn't fail her now.

As she strolled down Laurier Avenue, Grace appreciated the newly green-leafed, tree-covered street. She approached the University of Ottawa campus and crossed the street, drawn to the familiarity of the place. Skirting the edges, the memories flowed back. Taking classes had been hard work, but she'd lived at home with both Mom and Dad and life had been pretty simple then.

"How was school today, honey?" her mom had asked.

"Fine, but I can't stand my economics professor. He is not only dry and boring, but he's arrogant too."

"A lovely combination in a professor, I'm sure." Mom had laughed, picked up the tea towel she'd dropped, and headed back to the kitchen, calling over her shoulder, "Eat, eat. You must be starving."

Thinking back to how little she'd helped around the house shamed her. Mom and Dad would talk and laugh together in the kitchen while she sat on the couch watching television. She hadn't known how good she'd had it.

Getting choked up, Grace jogged back to the main street to get some distance from the emotions threatening to knock her to her knees. She shoved them to the back of her mind. It was a beautiful day. She'd had a beautiful mother who had loved her, and that was more than some ever had. Dad, well, she and her dad would get back on track when she was ready. Grace knew he was just waiting for that call but wasn't pushing her to make it.

Crossing the Rideau Canal, she looked down at the walkers and joggers making their way along the paths on either side. A tour boat had just come up the locks from the Ottawa River, and the tourists were pointing animatedly this way and that. It was early June, and tourist season was already in full swing. She loved June. Everything was so fresh and clean, and the entire summer lay ahead. *To new beginnings*, Grace mentally toasted herself while inhaling the sweet-smelling air.

A jog would have done wonders to get rid of some nerves, but not knowing when her next shower would be, she settled for a brisk walk. Her body was still as strong as it had been when she had rowed. Stress being a motivator, Grace would use the rowing machine in their condo daily. A typical workout was a ten-minute piece to warm up the muscles followed by another ten to fifteen minutes of stretching. She always took her time stretching since it allowed her to avoid the pain of the upcoming workout for a few more minutes. Once she couldn't delay any longer, Grace would strap her feet in, grab the handle, make sure her shirt was tucked in so it didn't catch in the wheels of the seat, and then she would start pulling, slow and steady for half an hour. With the music blasting, she would lose herself in the rhythm. Once the first piece was done, Grace would get off the machine, stretch her back out, and then sit down to do it again. Grace was a creature of habit. And exercise, like her journal, kept her sane.

Walking down the canal toward Dow's Lake, Grace enjoyed the opportunity to stretch her legs and watch the faces of the people coming toward her. The normal, happy— or at least, mostly happy—people. It gave her hope. Briefly making eye contact with a man in his late twenties—he wore a suit and sat on a bench talking on his phone—she glanced away but felt his eyes on her back as she walked past. Yesterday, Grace would have been in trouble for the eye contact, had *he* seen. The guy might've been in physical danger had it come to more than that. Feeling a rush of freedom at her moment of rebellion, Grace knew she was no longer under his rule. She'd broken free.

Having walked the three miles to the lake, Grace found a bench at its edge and sat for a few minutes. It was a new day. A new beginning. And as she let her gaze fall on the ripples on the water, she said a silent prayer, hoping she was right. Looking at her watch, it was 11:15 already. She figured she had better get back to Elgin Street and have a bite to eat before her 12:30 check-in.

The thrill of the upcoming adventure and the safety it would provide, along with the fear of missing the bus, pumped through Grace as she jogged back up the path. She couldn't help herself; it was worth getting a little sweaty. Making her way up Elgin to The Lieutenant's Pump, she realized too late that she would have to pass the police station. Heart pounding, she pulled her cap low, hunched her shoulders, and changed her gait so that she walked with a slight limp. She had met a few of his friends with the Ottawa Police Service and wasn't taking any chances.

Arriving at The Pump, Grace scanned the mostly empty bar and relaxed as she walked into the dim, cool room. She'd always loved the low, red upholstered booths, dark wooden tables, and extravagant bar with the long handles behind the counter used to pour the pints. Plus, she loved the smell of hops. Sitting at a booth with her back to the wall, Grace treated herself to a pint of Alexander Keith's and a burger. Who knew when she would get to have a beer or a good burger again. She wasn't sure what the food would be like over the next week. As she ate, she noticed people with backpacks and pillows arriving alone or with a partner. Some ate, some ordered a drink or a pop. Eyes down, Grace continued eating.

Two men walked in, chatting to one another. One was tall and willowy with shiny, jet-black hair, short in the back but parted to the side and longer in the front. He wore hiking boots, neatly pressed jeans, and a white, long-sleeved cotton shirt pushed up partway to the elbow. There was a logo over his chest on the left she couldn't quite make out. Flipping his hair out of the one eye, he looked down at his clipboard. The other man was older and heavier set. His face more serious, lined with age, the elements, and life experience. He stood with his hands in his pockets, took a step back, and called out, "Who is here for the artists' retreat with Northern Adventure Tours?"

Grace tentatively raised her hand along with the rest. She noticed two couples and two single women. One couple was a little older, and she found herself hoping they were up for the hiking and canoeing and the general lack of comfort for the week. The other two were in their mid-twenties, like herself, but were a whole different kind of artistic. They had an obvious love of tattoos and piercings and were all about self-expression and each other, apparently, as they shared an embarrassingly long kiss while he held her with one arm and the guitar on his back in place with the other.

The two women were as different as they could be. One was in her fifties and was tall, dark, and elegant with an intense and independent air. The other was small with shoulder-length, white-blond curly hair, funky red glasses, and a big grin.

For the second time today, Grace felt eyes on her. She searched the room for their source. Her heart stopped. It was a face she had seen only once before, but a face she'd thought of often in her darker moments. The memory of a single dance had held her up like a life preserver and kept her from going under over and over. It was a face she hadn't expected to see again. Grace had no idea where he was from or even his name, but there he was at the bar holding his glass and staring at her with those calm green eyes.

Quickly looking away, she told herself that he probably didn't even remember who she was. When she looked over again, he was sipping his beer and studying the bar top in front of him. He was every bit as unsettling as he'd been that night so long ago. Tall with wide shoulders and a graceful, athletic build. She remembered his light brown hair cropped close and eyes that had twinkled with humor and intelligence. But that was then. Who knows where his life had taken him. He likely had someone special in his life, and Grace was sure that talking with him now wouldn't be the same.

That door had closed, she told herself, and thank goodness for that. She was not ready to open a new door yet. Having just left a relationship yesterday, her door was shut, locked, and bolted for good measure. Her bruised heart thumped sporadically in relief.

Grace finished her burger as she listened to the man speaking in the middle of the bar.

"Okay, I am Cody Thompson, and this is Louis Dumais. I am the organizer of this outfit, and Louis is our Algonquin Provincial Park subject-matter expert, otherwise known as our APP-SME," he said with a wide grin. Looking down at his clipboard, he continued, "Okay, let's see who is who. Nicki Clark?"

The smiling blonde put up her hand.

"Jim and Evelyn Graham?"

The older couple.

"Margot Bouchard?"

The severe but elegant woman dressed in loose-fitting beige linen pants with a drawstring at the waist. She wore a black cotton tank top with a complicated-looking camera hanging around her neck. Obviously, a photographer. She nodded, her gray-streaked curls bouncing as she did.

"Katherine Green and Jake Evans?" he asked, looking toward the younger couple.

He gave a very cool wave, she a wink.

"Call me Kat," she said, hand on hip.

"That leaves Cam," he said, turning and pointing to the man at the bar. "Cameron Scott, right?"

"Yep, that's me," he confirmed.

Hm. So, that was his name, Grace thought.

"And, last but not least, Grace Rhodes?" Cody looked her way, and she nodded.

"Thankfully, Grace called this morning to fill Cam's pal's desertion."

"Hey, you can't blame the guy. His wife went into labor four weeks early," Cam lightheartedly defended his absent friend.

"Serves him right leaving her to go on a trip when she's so pregnant," Nicki teased.

"Well, I see your point, but she was the one who surprised him with the trip," Cam rebutted with a shrug. "She said he should get away for one more fishing trip before the baby comes."

"Wow, where'd he get a wife like that? And does she have a sister?" Cody winked at Grace.

Ha-ha. She grimaced.

With a clap of his hands, Cody shouted, "Okay, let's get everyone on the bus!" He smiled around the room, then, remembering something, said, "It'll be a little tight. There isn't any storage underneath, so you'll have to put your bags under your feet or on your lap."

Groans flooded the space until Louis said, "We didn't say this was a luxury cruise. Trust me, the three hours of discomfort will be worth it."

"Settle your tabs, use the restroom, and we'll see you on the bus. We leave in ten minutes." Cody walked over to Grace's table, then held out his hand. Grace swallowed down her barely chewed food and wiped her hand on her napkin before accepting the handshake.

"Hi, Grace. Nice to meet you." His grip was firm, his hands callused. The hands of a working man.

"Uh, nice to meet you too." Grace took a sip of beer to wash down the last of her lunch. Reaching for her purse, she said, "I think I owe you some money."

"How did you want to pay for the trip? A check will do just fine if that works for you."

"Would it be okay if I paid you cash?" she whispered, eyebrows raised.

He tilted his head to the side. "Uh, sure, but that's a lot of money to be carrying around."

"Yes, I know," she said, waiting until the last stragglers had left before counting out the money from the thick envelope. "I just moved to the city and I haven't gotten my checks in the mail yet."

He nodded, shoving his hands in his pockets. His biceps caught her attention for a moment. "Where'd you move from?"

"Peterborough."

"Oh, did you go to school there?"

"No, I went to college here and then moved there for a job." She finished off the last of her beer and pushed the glass away.

"Where did you work?" he asked.

"I worked at a bank there." *Please stop asking me questions.*

"What's your degree in?"

"Business."

"Hm. Well, glad you're here, Grace." Although the obvious next question would be why she had moved back, good manners finally stopped him. Thankfully, she had been able to tell the truth. One misdirection becomes a small fib, which will inevitably become a lie. Each lie becomes bigger and bigger until you just can't be yourself. She had hated that. Grace hated that *he* had put her in that position so often over the last couple of years. She used to be an open book.

Now Grace felt she just made people uneasy. They could see the conflicting emotions on her face. Some people wanted to get to know her better, but they sensed her discomfort and kept their distance.

"Well, we had better get on the bus," Cody said with a reserved smile.

"Yes, I will be right there. I just have to pay for my meal."

Going to the cash register to pay, she asked for her bill and found that it had already been paid. She asked who paid for it.

"The guy at the bar."

Slinging the backpack over her shoulder, Grace hurried to get out to the bus and discovered she was the last to get on. A ten-passenger van for ten people, their luggage, and a guitar wasn't roomy—it was downright squishy. There were two seats at the front with two seats behind them. The third row had a little aisle with a third spot, and then in the very back row were three more slightly larger seats.

The two men running the camp were at the front with Louis at the wheel. The young couple was at the very back with Margot. The older couple, Jim and Evelyn, was in the front row, and Nicki sat in the single seat in front of Margot. Cam sat across the aisle from her. Shit. She was going to have to sit beside him, the guy who had just bought her lunch, who absolutely crackled with a cuteness that she was not ready for or entitled to.

Nicki, sensing Grace's discomfort, rescued her. She turned and spoke to him. "Hey, if I know men, and I think I do, as I have three at home, they all like their legroom. Why don't you take this spot?" Turning back to Grace, she continued, "Grace, is it?" She nodded. "You take the window in case you want a nap. I don't mind sitting in the middle if that's okay with the two of you."

Pressing her lips together Grace nodded and said, "Sure, that sounds good."

Grace took a step or two back to give Nicki and Cam a wide berth to exit. She stupidly smiled at the ground, then stepped back up and into the van, quite aware that her butt was pretty much face level.

Red-faced, she shoved her backpack between her feet and hugged her sweatshirt to her chest. Shy on the best of days, she didn't want to be dealing with Cam right now. Grace wondered if she had made the right decision committing to being in such close quarters with people she didn't know.

Closing her eyes, she took a few deep breaths and told herself that they all seemed like reasonable people and there was always safety in numbers. *Unless your ex was a bipolar, trigger-happy cop.* Looking out the window, she worried that maybe she'd doomed this group. *But he wouldn't do anything in a group this size*, Grace thought. Then again, if he saw her this close to so many men, he'd go ballistic. Who knew what he was capable of?

The bus took a left across traffic, and Grace warily looked at the police station on their right as they drove by. Her sweatshirt had moved up to cover her nose, and she caught Cam glancing at her with curiosity—and maybe a little worry—as he followed her eyes out the window toward the police station.

Great, now he probably thinks I'm a criminal escaping some big heist. Grace hugged herself and looked out her window, not really seeing anything, and was thankful when Nicki pulled out a paperback and started to read. Cam had stretched his long legs out in front of him, arms crossed and eyes closed.

The couple behind her was discussing a performance last night at one of the local pubs and how it had been a bigger crowd than usual. He'd tried out a new song or two, and they had been well received.

Grace missed hanging out with friends at a pub. That's where she'd met *him*, but he soon began to insist he preferred to stay at home with her. That didn't stop him from heading to the bar after a shift with his buddies, and she often wondered what kept him out so late some nights. Grace refused to consider where he was and certainly couldn't discuss it with him. That would go nowhere and end up with her in the wrong, because she was "so jealous and insecure." Jealous and insecure? That had never been her. Maybe the loss of her mother had brought it on, he'd suggested, and said that he understood but she should really try to control it. The green-eyed monster didn't look good on her, he'd said.

She was exhausted. Exhausted by years of mind games. She'd slept fitfully the night before as the swirling negativity had clouded her thoughts, even in sleep. Glad Nicki had suggested the window, Grace closed her eyes and tried to ignore the perfume coming from the seat behind. The scent was beautiful but strong.

Grace absentmindedly listened to Jim and Louis talking about the forecast for the week, 75 to 85 degrees Fahrenheit and sunny. She didn't have sunscreen or bug spray. Although Nicki, mom of two, with the extra bag, would have some, and something told Grace that she'd be happy to share. There was comfort in that; she could use some motherly companionship.

Nicki had turned in her seat and was chatting with Margot, who responded with a gravelly voice. They had found some common ground in gallery talk. Grace wondered if she would be out of her element when it came to discussions on art. Although she had an appreciation for it, she had never studied it or even discussed it with anyone, let alone made it her profession.

Trying again to tune it all out to get some rest, Grace only succeeded in getting a headache from her head bouncing on the window, coupled with the perfume. Giving up, she sat up and looked out the window to see where they were. No longer in the city, the van was flying along the highway heading west toward Algonquin Park. The pamphlet had said it was a three-hour drive, and they were maybe only an hour in. Grace pulled out the pamphlet to take a better look at what she'd gotten herself into. It read:

Escape to God's Country.

Dumais Lodge is located on Thompson Lake, which was leased from the federal government by Cody Thompson's great-great-grandfather, John Charles Thompson, in 1929 as a family getaway. Over time, they developed the property to make it more comfortable for family and friends. Cody started Northern Adventure Tours when he discovered the need for people to escape the pressures of the city and day-to-day life. Cody runs the lodge with Louis Dumais, a trusted family friend, naturalist, guide, chef, and fisherman.

__Main Lodge__ — The main lodge contains a large kitchen, dining area, and lounge as well as restrooms with showers.

Cabins — There are two cabins located near the main lodge. You are welcome to a tent if you prefer. Tents, bedding, and extra blankets are available upon request.

Hiking Trails — We have access to beautiful hiking trails and logging roads near the lodge that you may use at any time. We will be canoeing and boating to other locations with more challenging trails and opportunities for fishing and inspiration depending on your interests.

Beach — There is a lovely beach just down from the lodge next to the firepit area. The beach has a sand bottom out to about 20 feet, where there is a sharp drop-off. Swim with care and never alone.

Firepit — There will be nightly campfires. We encourage you to join in and get to know your fellow campers. Bring a blanket from your cabin, lean back in one of our gorgeous Adirondack chairs, and stay up late to watch the beautiful aurora borealis dance across the night sky.

Meals — Louis Dumais, our own Red Seal–certified chef, will be preparing a variety of delicious meals daily.

Itinerary

<u>Day One</u>

1:00 P.M. — *Leave Ottawa
(The Lieutenant's Pump)*
4:00 P.M. — *Arrive at Thompson Lake/
Dumais Lodge*
6:00 P.M. — *Dinner*
9:00 P.M. — *Campfire*

<u>Day Two</u>

8:00 A.M. — *Breakfast*
9:00 A.M. — *Canoe to Inspiration Point*
Noon — *Shore lunch*
1:00 P.M. — *Personal time*
4:00 P.M. — *Canoe back to lodge*
6:00 P.M. — *Dinner*
9:00 P.M. — *Campfire*

<u>Day Three</u>

8:00 A.M. — *Breakfast*
9:00 A.M. — *Personal time at
Thompson Lake*
Noon — *Lunch*
1:00 P.M. — *Boat to natural waterslides*
4:00 P.M. — *Boat back to lodge*
6:00 P.M. — *Dinner*
9:00 P.M. — *Campfire*

Day Four

8:00 A.M. — Breakfast
9:00 A.M. — Hike the logging trail
Noon — Shore lunch
1:00 P.M. — Personal time
4:00 P.M. — Hike back to lodge
6:00 P.M. — Dinner
9:00 P.M. — Campfire

Day Five

8:00 A.M. — Breakfast
9:00 A.M. — Canoe to Moose Bay
Noon — Shore lunch
1:00 P.M. — Canoe to Painted Cliffs
4:00 P.M. — Canoe back to lodge
6:00 P.M. — Dinner
9:00 P.M. — Campfire

Day Six

8:00 A.M. — Breakfast
10:00 A.M. — Bus leaves for Ottawa

As Grace read the itinerary, she began to imagine the week ahead. She couldn't wait for the long canoe trips and hikes during the day and sitting around the campfire at night. And there was enough personal time that the group thing shouldn't wear her down too much.

Noticing what she was looking at, Nicki asked, "Looks like fun, huh?"

Grace nodded. "Yeah, it does."

"Just what I need." Nicki smelled of soap, with a hint of lemon.

"Me too." Grace smiled.

"Are you an artist?"

"Well, no, I can't really say that I am. I like art, but this is more of . . . an escape for me. It'll be nice to spend some time away from the city." Grace paused. "I've wanted to get away for a long time now, and when I stumbled across this pamphlet, it seemed like the perfect opportunity. What about you?"

"I paint." Nicki's bright blue eyes sparkled beneath her red, horn-rimmed glasses. "I got back into it when the boys were both in school."

Nodding, Grace glanced at Nicki from the corner of her eye. "How often are you able to commit to it?"

The van bounced through a particularly large pothole, and they both grabbed the seat backs in front of them. "Well, I work a couple days a week, and between that and getting errands done, I usually have one or two days to work on my art before the family is home for the weekend."

Shrugging, she said, "I don't have a lot of time, but it's enough. Consistency is the thing."

"Sounds great." Her smile wavered as she remembered bright Sunday mornings when the smell of freshly brewed coffee would waft into her room and tickle her nose, peeking out from beneath her down comforter.

"There are times I am inspired and do more." Her words came tumbling out as she spoke. "In the summer, for example, when there are fewer activities and longer daylight hours. This trip will kind of kick-start things for me. I'll paint while I'm here, but I'll take a lot of pictures too and save them to paint later."

Nicki sounded so happy, so normal. What could Grace say? *"I am jobless. My ex is searching high and low so that he can kill me because he always promised he would if I left. My mom died, and my dad has new stepchildren who allow him to forget about me and pretend the pain of his past doesn't exist."*

Grace smiled wistfully, eyes blurring.

Nicki knew that something was wrong but didn't press Grace with questions. A crowded van wasn't the place to discuss it.

Grace liked her for that.

The conversation in the front stopped at that same moment, and the guitar being strummed in the back seat became more noticeable. They listened as the song transitioned into one Grace knew well.

Jake started singing, softly at first, then, as he saw encouraging nods, he began to sing a little louder. Those who could sing joined in, and Grace couldn't help but smile at everyone bonding for the first time. She turned to look at Jake, who was focused on his fingers, then looked up to smile back at Kat. At the front of the bus, she saw Louis bobbing his head to the music. Cody's teeth flashed white against his olive skin as he looked back over his shoulder at the new crew. Nicki clapped to the music, Jim and Evelyn sang along, and Margot had a pleasant smile on her face as she gazed out the window. Grace avoided looking past Nicki to Cam, but as she was half-turned in her seat, she noticed Cam glance at her from the corner of his eye. Did he remember her? If so, he was probably wondering what had happened to that happy, confident girl he'd danced with. Shaking her head, Grace gazed out the window and questioned: *How did I get here?*

CHAPTER 4

I Went to the Woods

—Henry David Thoreau

THEY ROLLED UP TO THOMPSON LAKE AT FOUR O'CLOCK, right on schedule, and were welcomed by a long-legged, gray-and-white dog named Wolf. Quite sure that he was part wolf, despite his bright blue eyes, they kept a wary eye on him as they gingerly stepped out of the van and straightened themselves after the long bus ride. The air was fresh and moist, the smell of pine overpowering, all contributing to the magic of the place. Listening to the murmurs of delight from the other guests, Grace was drawn toward the lake by a red canoe slowly moving in the distance.

"Make yourselves at home," Cody called to the group behind her. "Have a bio break—the bathrooms are just through the front door of the lodge on your right—and we'll meet at the picnic tables in the camp kitchen in fifteen minutes."

Relieved to have a few minutes on her own, Grace stretched her arms overhead and bent side to side.

"Beautiful," Grace heard someone say from behind her.

She jumped and spun as though to face an attacker but saw it was Cam walking toward her.

"Seriously?" she said a little more harshly than she meant to, wondering whether he'd been referring to the scenery.

"Sorry, I didn't mean to startle you."

Grace muttered, "I've been a little jumpy lately."

Cam stuffed his hands in his pockets, not knowing what to say.

Grace wondered if he remembered her. She couldn't tell.

Crossing her arms, head tilted, she asked, "Hey, did you pay for my lunch?" To his smile and nod, she continued, "You didn't have to do that."

"My pleasure."

"I guess I owe you one."

"A fresh cup of coffee in the morning would be wonderful," he teased.

"Deal," Grace promised with a soft smile. It felt strange to talk to a man; it was strange to talk to anyone, really. She hadn't even seen her dad for a couple of months. Not since she had hurt her hand. She hadn't wanted him to ask any questions.

People had started to wander toward the picnic tables, so Grace excused herself to run to the restroom before she missed the opportunity. As she jogged to the main lodge, her heart soared at the thought of five nights in this beautiful place. Her excitement had nothing to do with the man behind her, she told herself.

They huddled in and around the camp kitchen. It was built of rounded logs, much like the surrounding buildings, and had open-air windows on the two lengths and back of the building with a large opening at the front for entry. Inside was a picnic table and a wood-burning stove vented to the ceiling with a rough black pipe. A pile of birch firewood lay beside it.

"We call this the camp kitchen. It's nice to have on a rainy day." Cody pointed to the roof before thumbing to the area behind him. "There are two cabins—or bunkhouses as some like to call them—and the main lodge. There's a cabin for the men and another for the women, but if the couples want to be together, we have tents, so just let us know."

Evelyn shook her head. "No, thank you. I could use a night without *someone's* snoring."

Cradling the clipboard in his arm, he ran his finger down the list and skimmed his notes. "The main lodge has two restrooms and shower areas. There are towels and washcloths and a hamper for when you're finished." A woodpecker *rat-tat-tatted* in the distance, the sound echoing across the lake. "There are enough lockers for everyone, but unfortunately, we don't have any locks. So, keep your personal items close if you're worried about losing them."

"If they go missing, don't worry, we will likely find the culprit," Louis said with a wry smile.

"That being said . . ." Cody stepped back so he could see everyone. "We have a few rules and housekeeping items that we should go over." Counting each on a finger, he said, "One, try to stay together. You may take a break from the group on our outings, when you work on your art, but don't go swimming or hiking on your own. Two, don't leave food unattended. It will attract the wildlife. Three, always lend a helping hand. We don't want to have to micromanage the week. If you see a job that you don't mind doing, jump in and do it. Campfire builders may not like to fillet fish, and toilet bowl cleaners may not like to do dishes. Help where you can.

"Louis is a mean cook. He will be making full meals each evening. He prepares the food during the day while you're on your personal time but would love help setting the table and cleaning up afterward.

"There is bedding on each bunk. If you need an extra pillow, help yourself. There should be more in the closet.

"There are two washers and two dryers in the lodge. If you're planning to do laundry, sign up and make sure you don't leave your laundry sitting in there wet. Be considerate."

He looked away from his clipboard, then eyed the group. "No drugs." Some snickered.

"Alcohol. Well, did you bring any? No? Not to worry, there will be wine and beer available every evening with dinner. Just keep in mind that we have some early mornings and fairly aggressive canoes and hikes ahead of us, so a hangover won't help you through your day. And, given that this is an artists' retreat, I would bet it won't make you overly creative, either."

There were a few chuckles.

"So, go make yourselves at home. Find a bunk, settle in, and have some quiet time if you like. Louis and I will start supper. When you're ready, come up to the lodge for happy hour."

The women and their luggage merged at the doorway to their cabin. It was sparse but roomy. There were four sets of bunk beds, one on each wall. Kat ran for the farthest one. "I call top bunk!" which suited Grace just fine; she was somewhat surprised to see Kat had joined the women. She thought Kat and Jake might want to be together.

Preferring the coziness, Grace grabbed a bottom bunk near the window facing the lake and activities. Evelyn said, "Oh, I'll take this one over here. It'll be nice and quiet, and this mattress looks comfy."

Nicki threw her bag under Kat's bunk, and Margot took the one nearest the door.

Stretching out felt great after the long bus ride and, closing her eyes, Grace again wondered what she'd gotten herself into.

"This is going to be heaven." Nicki sighed. "No lunches to prepare, no laundry to do, no homework to help with, or fights to stop. Oh, and I'll be able to sleep an entire night without anyone asking me to come sleep with them."

"I wouldn't count on that," Kat joked. "I think that Cody has his eye on you."

"Yeah, right. I think Cody probably has his eye on all the girls. Charming fella. But no, I don't think I have anything to worry about. Now you ladies, that's a different story."

"Oh, yes," Evelyn chirped. "If it wasn't for my Jim, I am sure I'd have to beat him off with a stick."

"Margot, what's your story? Are you married? Do you have a family?" Nicki asked.

Looking at her camera lens and cleaning it again, she answered, "No, I'm not married. No kids. I really don't have the patience for all that. But I've been with my partner, Giovanni, for, oh, twenty-five years or so."

"Wow, do the two of you have a home together?" Grace asked.

"Well," she explained, "we have two homes, side by side."

Laughing at their shocked expressions, she said, "We aren't the most conventional of couples. We are both pretty intense and need our space. Over the years, we've found it best to do our own thing during the week and have our Friday nights together, come hell or high water."

How unusual, Grace thought, *and lonely.* She didn't think she could do that. She'd either want to be completely on her own or spend more time than that together, but to each their own. *Good for them for finding something that works.* And really, she had no right to judge.

"Boundaries. Gio and I know one another now and realize that to make it work, we need to respect our individual needs." She paused as she adjusted something on her camera. Looking up, she added with a twinkle in her eye and a quick tilt of her head, "Mostly, we just need our space."

"What do you do for a living? Are you a photographer?" Evelyn asked.

Margot checked her camera again and then clicked and said "Gotcha!" at the same time.

She walked across the room and showed Evelyn the photograph she'd taken.

"Oh my! That's wonderful!" Evelyn cried, astounded. "That's the best picture I've had taken of me in years! You are a genius with that camera, Margot."

"I guess she answered your question." Kat hopped down from her bunk and leaned in to get a look.

"Ha, I guess she did." Evelyn examined the picture.

Straightening, Kat focused her attention on Margot. "Freelance or salary?"

"Salary, mostly. I work for the Canadian Tourism Commission but freelance whenever I can."

"So, are you here for business or pleasure?" Elbows out, Nicki twisted left and right, then put her hand on her lower back with a grimace. "My back is killing me from that drive."

"For a bit of both, it would appear," she said, smiling broadly.

"Speaking of pleasure, I do believe I am going to head in for happy hour," Nicki announced. "Anyone care to join me?"

"A splendid idea." Evelyn slowly pushed herself up off her mattress and walked with Kat to the door of the cabin. Margot excused herself to go take some pictures, and Grace decided to stay in the cabin for a while and regroup. She pulled out her journal to try to get some perspective.

Tuesday, June 9th

I woke up this morning and made the rash decision to go on a canoe/camping trip geared for artists. I am

43

not an artist but will pose as one in order to hide from Psycho Cop for a few days. The thought of him makes me sick to my stomach. I'm trying not to show it, but I'm terrified. I don't know if or how I will ever get away from him. Maybe if I'm able to stay off his radar for long enough, he'll calm down, mellow out, and find some other poor woman to trap.

She stopped writing there. If he moved on, someone *else* would have to suffer as she had. And possibly not be lucky enough to escape. Grace knew then she had to do more than hide. She needed to find a way to stop him.

The smell of roast beef filled her nose as she stepped into the lodge. The dining room table sat empty, so Grace followed the voices into a rugged living space filled with various styles of furniture. There were stacking chairs with silver legs and white plastic seats that a few sat on. Others were settled more comfortably on ornate wooden chairs from someone's old dining room table. All the chairs were taken when Grace arrived, so Cam stood and offered his. However, instead of returning with the chair he had found in the corner, he joined Kat and Jake, who were sitting on their own. Grace glanced over and saw that Kat was sitting in a big, green, oversize chenille armchair. It had seen better days, but she looked like the queen of this castle and kingdom. Her gaze fell to the windows and the wild splendor beyond.

Grace couldn't help but feel it was a slight that Cam had sat where he did but tried not to let it bother her as she settled into her seat. Cody pulled a bottle of Coors Light out of an ice bucket sitting on the floor beside him and held it up to see if she would like one. Nodding, she listened to the conversation as Cody twisted off the lid and passed it to her.

"Do you get tired of the routine up here?" Nicki asked, taking a sip of her beer.

"Not really." Cody shook his head. "I suppose, like any job, you need a break from time to time. It does feel good to head to the city and see a movie and go to a restaurant. But eventually, the crowds start getting to me and it's time to head back up here."

"We aren't far from town—twenty minutes, and we're there." Louis shrugged. "We catch up with the gossip and see some family, so it isn't really as isolated as it seems."

"But week after week, doing the same thing? Going to the same locations?" she persisted, jutting her chin forward, hand held up in front of her, laughter in her eyes.

"Nope, not a problem." Louis pushed his chair back, stretching his legs out in front of him. He leaned into the chair and rested the back of his head in the palms of his intertwined hands. "Every day is surprisingly different. If the weather is bad, we have a movie night or host a poker tournament. Now and then, we set up a treasure hunt for something different to do."

"A treasure hunt?" Evelyn's voice was raised with interest.

"We bought a couple of Garmin handheld GPSs that we use to find boxes that we've hidden around the property."

Margot sat tall in her chair. "How does it work?"

"We start at a box near the camp kitchen. When you open it, there's a piece of paper giving you the coordinates to the next box. You plug the coordinates into the GPS and then follow the screen, which maps out which way to go. As you near the location of the next box, you need to look for it, as it will be hidden under the brush or in a hole in a tree."

Cam nodded. "I've heard of this. The boxes are usually camouflaged, so they're difficult to see."

Jim rubbed the back of his neck. "Don't you have to take something from the box and leave something?"

"Yes." Louis stood to head into the kitchen, his voice rising as he walked. "Technically. Although we don't bother with that here."

Grace leaned forward in her chair. "What kinds of things do people take or leave?"

"Stickers, badges, crayons. It depends on who the audience is." Cody shrugged. "If it's primarily adults who would be finding the caches, what's in it might be different than if it's geared for kids."

"Sounds fun," Evelyn said.

"Well, maybe we will have to do some geocaching this week." Cody took a sip of his drink.

Hearing Louis rummaging around in the kitchen, Grace went to see if she could help.

She took in the dining room table that had already been set and the macaroni salad that sat on the counter, still covered with plastic wrap. "You must have been up early today."

46

Raising his head to see who had come in, Louis looked back down and continued to slice some cheese to add to the tray of pickles. "No earlier than normal. I rise with the birds. Always have." Surveying the roast beef in the Crock-Pots and buns on the counter by the sink, he shrugged. "It didn't take much. I just threw the roasts in the slow cookers before we left."

"What can I do?" Grace asked, hands on hips.

"Why don't you assemble the Caesar salad? The romaine lettuce is ready to go—rinsed, torn, and patted dry. It's in the fridge. Grab the dressing while you're there. I stuck a sticky note on the jar." He nodded to the fridge to his left. "There's a big bowl in the bottom of that cupboard over there." He gestured toward it with his chin. "And the croutons will be coming out of the oven in just a minute."

As Grace mixed the salad, she inhaled the tangy lemon and creamy garlic dressing. Louis set a block of Parmesan cheese and a small cheese grater on the counter next to her before returning with the warm croutons. She gave it a final toss with the wooden artisan bear paws before adding a little more Parmesan on top. Carrying the big, wooden salad bowl on her hip as she walked, she set it at the end of the long dining room table. Moving toward the middle of the table, she claimed a spot by setting her beer bottle next to the glass for water.

"What do you use to fill the water glasses?" Grace scanned the large kitchen. "Oh, these must be them." She walked toward the two large pitchers sitting on the counter.

As she ran the water in the sink until it ran cold, she smiled at Louis as he dinged a tiny little triangle. "Ding, ding, ding . . . supper is served!" he shouted to those in the other room.

As the crowd made their way to the dining table with their drinks, Louis quickly pulled out a roast and started slicing it while Cody took the cheese and pickle tray and macaroni salad to the table.

"Nicki, can you grab the buns and butter, please?" Louis called to her as she came into the room. Grace walked to the table with her, a pitcher of water in each hand.

Cody stepped outside to call Margot while the rest settled in and chatted. Louis made his way to the table with the platter of roast beef as Margot and Cody came in and each grabbed a chair and sat down.

"If you don't mind, I would like to say a prayer that my mother taught me." Louis stood at the head of the table. "We thank the Great Spirit for the resources that made this food possible. We thank the Earth Mother for producing it. We thank all those who labored to bring it to us. May the wholesomeness of the food before us bring out the wholeness of the Spirit within us."

What a lovely prayer, Grace thought, as she grabbed a bun and filled it with roast beef from the platter that was being passed down the table.

"Margot, what do you do for a living?" Jim asked.

"She's a photographer," Evelyn chimed in, nodding knowingly.

Margot smiled. "Yes, I am a photographer by profession." She chewed, then swallowed. "I travel to places that are fairly remote, all around the world, and attempt to capture the landscape and the cultures and customs of the people."

"Very cool. That is my dream job. Where do I sign up?" Cody chuckled.

Margot smiled. "Well, how about I give you a few tips this week?"

Cody gave a single nod. "You're on."

Jim leaned across Evelyn to reach the salt. "Where all have you gone?" He opened his bun and salted his roast beef.

Evelyn leaned back, looked heavenward, and whispered, "Jim, *your blood pressure . . .*" She sighed.

"I've traveled extensively through Europe, often with Giovanni, but the last few years I've fallen in love with South America, specifically Brazil, Argentina, Colombia," she held her bun to her mouth and took a big bite.

At the far end of the table, Jake, Kat, and Cam burst out laughing at whatever it was they were talking about. The noise startled Grace, causing her to splash water on the table as she went to set her glass down. She glanced at Kat's nose ring and Jake's floppy hair and tattoos. They seemed so happy. Cam too—he had such an easy grin. She took another bite of her sandwich.

Why did he have to be here, anyway? Really, of all the people who could be on this trip. Well, she would just ignore him. Half turning in her seat, she casually reached for more salad, focusing her attention on Margot, Evelyn, and Nicki instead.

"Help yourself to dessert, everyone," Cody called from the kitchen. "It's chocolate cake—and not from a box!"

As others made their way to the kitchen, Grace remained seated, finishing her salad.

"Grace, aren't you having any cake?" Louis asked in his wise and quiet way, offering her one of the pieces that he had brought back.

"Thank you," she replied, taking it.

Chocolate cake had been one of *his* favorites. Getting groceries had been something to look forward to, so she had made the trip to the store almost daily and cooked whatever had spoken to her on that day. It was one thing she knew would put him in a good mood. Grace promised herself to study the meal plan for the week and try to replicate it when she found somewhere she could call home . . . and had furnished it with money that she did not yet have.

Feeling sick at the journey ahead, Grace looked down at her plate as tears pricked her eyes. Cam frowned in concern. "Grace, are you all right?"

She cleared her throat and tucked her hair behind her ear. "I'm not feeling well. Excuse me." Grace pushed her chair back, the sound of wood scraping floor alerting everyone to her exit. All eyes on her and heart thumping, she walked out of the dining room toward the back door of the lodge with as much composure as she could muster, knowing that some fresh air would help. Outside, she stumbled in her haste, wanting to put some distance between herself and the lodge. Hearing the creak of the springs on the lodge door, she started into a jog, hoping whoever it was would be discouraged from following.

The path that left the campsite on the other side of the camp kitchen looked to be a well-worn trail that ran parallel to the lake. Trees blocked the view of the water, so Grace focused on the path in front of her. The footsteps were louder now, so she ran faster, sweat beading on the nape of her neck. As she sprinted, though, she felt silly running away. *Honestly, what am I running from?* She slowed to a walk, then heard the footsteps again. Catching her breath, Grace wheeled around to face whoever had the nerve to infringe on her privacy. Surprise, surprise, it was Cam with Wolf loping beside him. Grace glared at him, arms crossed, as he trotted toward her, a sheepish grin spreading across his face.

Cam held his hands in the air, palms toward her. "Look, I don't want to pry."

"Then don't," she spat back as Wolf licked her hand.

"Hey, I don't need to know what's bothering you," he said, his voice rising. "I just don't want you to be on your own." He paused. "Having company might help. Besides, you're breaking rule number one."

"I'm tired of rules," she growled, continuing to walk, the small stones on the path grinding under her feet.

"They aren't *my* rules . . ." Cam walked alongside her, and they listened to the rhythm of their footsteps. "I wonder what the punishment is if you don't follow them." Cam lowered his brows in mock concern.

Grace tried to suppress a grin. Consciously releasing the tension in her neck and shoulders, she offered, "Getting eaten by a bear?"

"Better than washing toilets."

"Oh, don't worry, you'll get your chance at toilets. I'll sign you up." Grace turned her head to give him a mischievous smile. She slowed to a stop.

He smiled and looked back along the road they had just come down. She wasn't ready to head back.

"Don't worry, it's no big deal. Nobody even noticed you left."

Grace raised an eyebrow.

"Okay, maybe they noticed, but they aren't judging. I think they were all just worried about you. Come on back. They're going to have a campfire tonight."

Since there really wasn't anywhere else to go, Grace shrugged and turned to walk back to camp. She wasn't going to find the answers to her problems out here.

CHAPTER 5

To Look through Each Other's Eyes

—Henry David Thoreau

A S THEY WALKED BACK INTO THE LODGE, EVERYONE WAS busy clearing the table, putting food away, and doing dishes. Grace walked into the kitchen, found a tea towel, and busied herself with the drying. No one paid her any mind.

The kitchen smelled of warm water and dish soap. Louis rinsed a glass before setting it in the dish rack on the counter. "Well, you might see the odd moose on the shore of a lake as you're canoeing." His wet hands dripped onto the floor as he turned to face Jim. "But they have great hearing and are usually well aware that you're in the vicinity long before you have a chance to spot them." Turning back to the sink, he grabbed a large pot and began to scrub. "They like to keep their distance, so often they move on before you get a chance to see them."

"That's okay by me!" Jim said. "They are massive beasts. I wouldn't want to try to outrun or outkick one." Jim winked at Evelyn as he set a dinner plate on the island.

Cody put a water jug in the fridge nearest the dining room, beside the containers filled with leftover roast. The kitchen was huge with lots of prep area, two gas ranges, and two refrigerators. The cupboards creaked as dishes were put away, and they tripped more than once on the raised linoleum, but the size and functionality made it easy for the large group to move around.

Grace glanced at an open door at the other end of the kitchen and saw what looked like a large pantry area. Cody noticed her gaze and guessed at her train of thought. "That's the pantry back there. See that cupboard with the lock?" When she nodded, he smiled as he filled the silverware drawer with spoons, knives, and forks after drying them. He slid the drawer shut. "That's where we keep the booze. If you want a drink, just let me know. We'll put it on your tab."

"Why are you telling *me* this?" Grace huffed with pretend offense. "Do I look like I need a drink?"

"Yes!" multiple voices chimed in together.

She rolled her eyes but had to smile.

With the kitchen clean, Grace strolled over to the campfire. She could smell the smoke from the fire, and as she sat, she detected the distinct scent of citronella. Smoldering mosquito coils burned at intervals between each chair that surrounded the crackling fire.

Kat and Jake were there already, visiting and talking about the upcoming week with Cody. Jake had his guitar on his lap. He turned a knob and then played a chord, continued the conversation, and then tuned the guitar some more. Watching them, Grace had to admit the couple was a perfect match of artistic flair and darkness. They wouldn't waste a moment of their lives and didn't appear to be afraid of much, either. Carefree and happy, they had a different measure of success and another set of rules to live by. Grace envied them—their attitude and ways—and wished she was a little more like them.

As Jake started strumming a tune, Nicki arrived and dragged an Adirondack chair closer before plunking herself down in it to listen. Grace was excited to hear what he would play. He was going to bring a lot to the week. Like art, she loved music but was not really knowledgeable of it. Never having made a playlist or spent time learning the lyrics, she couldn't speak to bands or themes in the songs but appreciated it just the same and knew what she liked and what she didn't. That's all that matters, really; there are no rules when it comes to these things, she assured herself.

As the camp members trickled in and gathered around the fire, Jake played some mainstream stuff and some oldies but goodies like Blue Rodeo and the Counting Crows. It fit the mood: laid-back and easy. Reflective. It took the group from their city ways and relaxed them into the ways of the wild. Nature and song. Grace closed her eyes and sighed.

Hearing the crunching of gravel, Grace opened her eyes to see Cam walking toward the fire from the men's cabin. Hands in his jeans pocket, serious-faced, he glanced at her across the fire before settling in beside Nicki. She turned her attention to Jake, who was explaining how he and Kat had met.

"It was in The Pump where we all caught the bus today that I saw this lady for the first time," he reminisced while still lightly strumming his guitar, fixing Kat with a look that would make weaker women swoon. "She was sitting at a table with some friends, and I was determined to get her attention, so I played a song."

"And he stared at me through that entire song." Kat looked at Jake through long lashes.

"Did it work?" Jim chuckled, looking at Evelyn.

"Well, if you call her walking right up to me at the end of the last chorus and planting a minute-long kiss on my lips in front of the entire pub 'working,' then, yes, I guess it did." He tipped his head back and gave a small laugh.

"And we've never been apart since." Kat threw an arm around Jake's shoulder.

"How long ago was that?" Evelyn reached down to throw a small branch into the fire.

"Two years," they said together.

"To the day?" Cam's eyes widened in mock surprise.

"Well, no, but close enough. It will be on Friday. That's what this trip is all about: a celebration." Kat planted a kiss on Jake's cheek.

"Play us the song!" Nicki encouraged. "It had to be a good one."

"Sure. It was 'Iris' by the Goo Goo Dolls. Here goes." Jake began singing.

Watching the fire, Grace felt herself relaxing as she listened to Jake sing. It was easy to picture them in the dancing flames, Kat's confident, impish, and bright nature pulled to his hurt but loving soul.

As the song ended and the notes faded away, they were all quiet, feeling the emotion and beauty of the song. The memories of times past.

Grace remembered back to another time, another song. The memory felt excruciatingly recent. The sharp details a reminder that had she chosen another path, it might have saved a lot of heartache. Grace raised her eyes and looked at Cam across the fire, his eyes filled with memory and understanding.

Cody cleared his throat, breaking the moment. Grace turned her head toward him and saw that his jaw was clenched. Shaking it off, he began with a loud, authoritative voice, "Welcome to the first campfire of this week's artists' retreat!"

Cheers and clapping followed his announcement.

"We're going to have an amazing five days here."

More clapping and whistling.

"You're going to eat better than you have in a while. You're going to sleep better than you have in a while. You're going to use your muscles more than you have in a while. Well, most of you anyway." Cody chuckled, glancing at Grace, her strong arms and legs hard to miss.

Grace blushed as she stared madly at the ground.

Louis stood tall, feet apart, hands held behind his back. "Given that the theme this week is an artists' retreat, we hope that the fresh air, exercise, and nature will inspire you to do your best artistic work while you're here." He lifted his heels and puffed out his chest as he spoke. "Be it writing the next big hit," he said, looking over at Jake, "or painting a masterpiece for the art gallery in Ottawa," he said as he looked at Nicki, "we hope this week brings out the best in all."

"At the start of each week, we like to do an icebreaker." Cody sat upright as he addressed the crowd.

To a chorus of groans, he waved his hands in front of him. "I know, I know, these are always painful but so is being overly polite, right?" He waited for a few nods. "We only have five days together, and the sooner we get to know each other, the better it'll be and the more fun we'll have." He paused. "So, the icebreaker that we like to do here is Two Truths and a Lie."

Grace inwardly swore.

"Do we all know how it works?" Cody asked, looking around the group sitting comfortably in their chairs. "No? Yes? Looks like some do, some don't. Okay. The way it works is that each person takes a turn and says two truths and a lie in whatever order you like, and then we vote on which is the lie."

Margot reclined in her chair, legs crossed, elbows resting on the chair's wide, flat arms. "It's a great way to get to know one another." A beautiful smile formed on her lips. "I'll go first if you like."

"Sure, that would be great." With a sweep of the arm, Cody said, "Take it away."

"Okay. So, as you know, my name is Margot." Composing herself, she took a full breath. "Here goes. One, I was born and raised in Canada, my father is French, but my mother is Italian." She gazed over the chairs that surrounded the fire into the dark trees beyond. "Two, I have traveled to over fifty countries in my life." Margot brought her focus back to the people sitting around her. "And three, I am terribly afraid of mice."

"You are totally French Italian. You are Italian but super pale," Kat shouted out.

"Absolutely," Jim said, "and we know that you've traveled extensively."

"Okay, let's vote," Cody instructed. "Who thinks Margot lied about her fear of mice?"

Five hands went up.

"About traveling to fifty countries?" Cody continued.

Three hands.

"And that she is French Italian?"

Grace put her solitary hand in the air.

"And you, Grace, are the winner," Margot confirmed. "*That* is the lie. I am completely French—only heavily influenced by the Italians." She grinned.

Cody turned to Grace. "Okay, winner goes next."

"Oh, no! I'm not ready. Can someone else go first?" Grace pleaded, hands clasped to her chest.

"Okay, we'll give you some time. Who's ready?" Cody waited for a taker.

Her heart started beating double time. Grace hated speaking in a group bigger than four. Bigger than two, if the truth be known.

Okay, that'll be a fall-back truth if I need it, she thought.

"I'll go next," volunteered Kat with a smile. "Hmmm . . . Okay. I love red wine. I hate snakes. And I have ten tattoos on my body."

"Okay, let's get the voting started." Cody rubbed his hands together. "Who thinks she actually hates red wine?"

No takers.

"Who thinks she loves snakes?" Again, five hands went up.

"And . . . who thinks she does not have ten tattoos on her body?"

The remaining four hands went up.

"And drumroll, please." Kat drummed the side of the chair for Cody. "The correct answer is . . . ?"

"I hate . . . red wine."

"What?! That's blasphemy!" Nicki cried. "What is *wrong* with you?" She shook her hands at Kat, then covered her face in mock horror.

Kat shrugged. "I never said I was normal."

"No winners on that one," Cody pronounced. "Grace, are you ready?" With a shake of her head, he looked around the campfire. "Jim."

"Well, now. I hate to give away all my secrets, but if it's okay with you, Evelyn, I guess I can share just a little." He drawled that last bit, then threw a playful, questioning glance at his wife.

"Of course." She smiled, happy to be asked.

"Well, I might have to suggest that she be removed from the voting, or this game will be null and void."

"Good point." Louis laughed. "I guess you can't vote this round, Evelyn."

"Fine with me."

"Wait a sec! Jake, you voted on Kat's turn!" Cody pointed at him.

"Yeah, I lied." Jake laughed and ran his hand through his hair.

"All righty. Well, three things about myself," Jim began. "I am recently retired from the Ontario Provincial Police. I am fifty-nine years old. And I have three children—two boys and a girl."

"That's a toughie," stated Cam, getting into the game. "You can't be fifty-nine. That's my vote."

"Who's with Cam? Jim isn't fifty-nine?"

Eight hands went up.

Chuckling, Jim said, "Right you are. I'm sixty. I just had my birthday last weekend."

"No way," Nicki said. "You look too young to be sixty."

"Damn birthdays," Kat said. "They're always making us feel bad."

"This is what I think about age," Jake interjected. "It doesn't mean crap. It's who you are inside that matters. Whether the knees creak or the hair grays, we are who we are. At any age."

"Cheers to that," agreed Evelyn, lifting an invisible glass in the air.

"Sounds like a hit. Keep working on that." Jim's cheeks went pink with pleasure. "Jake, why don't you take a turn?"

Jake paused. The mood changed as Jake bit his lip and looked at the ground, nodding to himself.

"Well . . ." He glanced at Kat. "There isn't anyone in the entire world that I like or love more than this lady here. My guitar speaks for my soul . . . and, um, well, I guess I am not very good at this game, but since I have to say one more thing . . . I'd love to see my dad for Christmas this year." He looked down at his guitar in embarrassment, his teeth flashing white with a half-smile.

"I guess it's obvious which the lie is." Kat leaned in and bumped Jake's shoulder with her own. "His dad's not the nicest of men."

There was a pause before Louis jumped in. "Thank you, Jake. This is what this game is for. Getting to know one another without pretense." He paused. "I love these weeks up here. I get to meet the most amazing and interesting people. We all have a skeleton in our closet, and sometimes it helps to hear that we aren't the only one. Thank you for sharing."

Feeling bad for Jake and thinking he had set the mood, Grace offered to take her turn.

"I think I'm ready now."

All eyes on her. What to say? Her heart raced.

"Two truths, one lie," she said, preparing herself. "Okay, sorry if I bum you all out, but here goes. One, my mother died of breast cancer less than a year ago." Grace kicked at a small rock in front of her. "Two, my dad has already moved in with another woman. And her kids." And, not knowing what she could lie about, she told a third truth.

"Three. I just ran away from my boyfriend two days ago. He has always threatened to kill me if I left, and he's a cop, so I'm pretty sure he'll find me."

Silence.

She grimaced, then her shoulders slumped. "Sorry, I played the game wrong. All true."

There was more silence until Nicki came and sat on the edge of Grace's chair and put her arm around her. "Thanks for letting us in on what you're going through. Things look pretty awful right now, but it'll be okay."

"Can we take a timeout?" Evelyn asked, giving Jim a wink. "I could use the bathroom."

And with that, Jake started another song to smooth things out.

Grace appreciated the gesture but grimaced at what Cam must be thinking. *Dodged a bullet with that crazy gal*, she would bet. Well, now he knows that she's damaged goods, and he'll back off.

Grace sat mortified that she had shared all her issues with a group of strangers and was furious for making herself look weak. She wanted to run and bury her head in a pillow, but that would make her look even more foolish. She wished she could leave the camp altogether, but where would she go? And so, Grace stared at the fire as it crackled and popped, pretending that what had happened hadn't. She listened to the sound of the guitar and tried to breathe the shame away. Nicki sat silently on the armrest of Grace's chair and rubbed her back, not saying anything.

Jim moved to the chair on the other side of Grace, put his elbows on his knees, held his hands together, and spoke quietly, "I don't want you to worry now, honey. We are going to take care of you. As you heard, I'm a retired Ontario Provincial Police officer, and even though I have turned in my badge, it's still a part of me. I still have friends on the force. Powerful ones. And we won't let this jackass touch you."

Grace looked up at him and felt the first glimmer of hope she'd had in a long time.

Grace lay on her back in the inky darkness of the cabin. The moon shone past the branches of the trees and through the window above her bed. She listened to Nicki's deep breaths and the whistle of Evelyn's stuffy snore. Grace had thought she would sleep well that night, but her mind kept flashing images from the last forty-eight hours. The trip to the city from Peterborough on the bus, the bed and breakfast, The Lieutenant's Pump, and now Thompson Lake and Dumais Lodge. The cabin smelled musky and damp, so she reached up and inched opened the window to let in some fresh air.

"Can't sleep?" came a voice from the blackness.

Grace lifted her head. "No. You neither?"

"Nope." Margot swung her legs out of bed and sat up. "I'm going to see if I can catch the northern lights. Would you like to join me?"

"Sure." Grace sat up and reached under her bunk for her sneakers and grabbed her hoodie.

They tiptoed to the door of the cabin, and the springs creaked as Kat rolled over. They waited to let her drift off before opening the door. Hearing her shallow breathing start again, Margot opened the door and they stepped out into the chilly night air.

Margot led the way to the beach, the scent of the campfire still lingering in the air. "We'll see them better on the water if they're out tonight."

Grace pulled her hands into her sleeves and rubbed her arms for warmth. "The moon looks bright even through the trees." The moon cast shadows of the long-armed trees on the ground.

"Yes." Margot nodded as she walked carefully, watching for tree roots poking out of the ground here and there. "I was hoping for a clear night."

Finding a canoe, they each grabbed a life jacket and dragged the boat to the water's edge. Margot stepped gingerly in and settled herself and her camera down while Grace gave the boat a shove off the sandy bottom and hopped in as it rolled free.

They moved through the dark waters in silence. Even the animals must be in bed for the night. The lake wasn't large, and the surface a mirror that reflected their movements as they reached for the next stroke. They heard every dip of their blades, as well as the water drops falling back down as they reached forward for yet another stroke.

"That should be good." Margot laid her paddle across the gunwales of the canoe, and it glided to a stop.

Following her lead, Grace set her paddle down and looked up into the sky. The tranquility of the lake settled all around them.

"There." Margot pointed back above the shore from which they had come. "Do you see that?"

An owl hooted as Grace looked in the direction she was indicating.

Sure enough, there was the faint green of the aurora borealis in the distance.

"I've never seen them before." Grace gazed in wonder as they shimmered. They weren't as vibrant as the pictures she'd seen and only covered a small portion of the sky, but they were magical.

"Neither have I." Margot lifted her camera and snapped a few pictures.

They watched, mesmerized, as the aurora moved in effortless motion across the canvas of the night sky, morphing from a swooping arch to a wide band of shimmering green, snaking its way to encompass more of the dark space above them. Closer now, it hovered over the canoe, creating a canopy that seemed so alive it appeared to catch the dreams of those who watched it. Or perhaps it contained the spirits of all those who have gone before and sends their messages. They spoke with a faint hum. Grace closed her eyes to listen and sensed their happiness, their contentment, their love of all that is life.

In a hushed voice, Margot spoke, still looking at the air above her. "They say the aurora borealis is created when the sun's particles travel through space and combine with the Earth's magnetic field. When the particles hit the atmosphere, they give up their energy to atoms and molecules of gases to create the colors found in the northern lights. Not only does this give us the beautiful colors, but if you're away from the city and other sounds, you can hear a faint hum or even a clapping sound."

"I thought I could hear it before, but it was very faint." They listened in silence.

"I guess with equipment, it sounds very much like someone turning a dial on an old A.M. radio. Depending on the night, the density of the particles, etcetera, there are many different sounds that are created." Margot spoke into the quiet of the night. Grace wished they could hear it better.

"The low-frequency electromagnetic waves whistle, growl, tweet. They can even sound like a group of otherworldly frogs singing a song."

Grace laughed to herself. "I'm sure they must have created some folklore around it."

"No doubt," Margot agreed. "The Earth is old, and I'm sure the borealis has been around for just as long."

Grace considered the magnitude of time and the immensity of the systems and galaxies beyond her own, and felt small. Insignificant. Strangely, it helped. Her problems seemed less important now.

"Oh! I think it's getting louder," Grace murmured more to herself than Margot. "It sounds more like a faint crackling now." Grace stared at the water in awe as she tried to keep from being distracted by the beauty of the ever-changing sky.

She heard a click. Margot had captured the moment. Grace was sure there had been a look of wonder on her face as she had listened. Easing herself down to the bottom of the canoe, she draped her legs over her seat and put her arms under her head and gazed upward at the soft beauty of the sky. Margot continued to capture it with her camera. Grace was content to record the experience in her mind, and as her eyes grew heavy, she allowed them to close and just listen to the beautiful sounds of Mother Earth.

Holding her hand to her breastbone, Margot let out a soft breath. "It's harder to spot the northern lights in June because the days are so long, especially in the far north."

On cue, they faded and were gone.

Margot took a few more pictures of the moon reflecting on Thompson Lake, the edge of the canoe with the moonlight reflecting on the water below and some of Dumais Lodge in moonlit shadow. Margot snapped the cover to the camera's lens back in place, and they headed for shore.

CHAPTER 6

Related to the Earliest Times, and to the Latest

—Henry David Thoreau

ONCE BACK IN BED, GRACE SLEPT WELL AND WOKE early. Having always been a morning person, her rowing days had cemented the wake-up trigger in her brain to ON when the clock struck five. She liked being the first one up, and although she was tired this morning, she enjoyed having the quiet time to herself.

Pulling on a sweatshirt and sneakers, she left the cabin and walked down toward the water, mesmerized by the sheer tranquility of the lake. It was so serene. Although the fresh air woke her a little, Grace decided a coffee was still in order. After dragging a chair onto the dock, she made her way to the main lodge to find some java.

It was dark and still in the lodge as she flipped on the light in the kitchen. Not wanting to wake Louis or Cody, who had their own rooms in the main building, Grace carefully opened cupboard doors until she found the coffee. Finding it, she filled the urn with water and put a generous amount of ground beans into the filter. It was a big pot for a big group, and she had no idea how much coffee would be enough. She hoped she hadn't made it too strong but figured there was nothing worse than a weak cup of joe. Flicking the switch to ON, Grace went to the bathroom to brush her teeth and hair while the coffee was brewing. Stepping out of the bathroom, lost in thought, she nearly jumped out of her skin as the door to the lodge opened beside her. A strong set of hands grabbed her shoulders and held her in place as the instinct to run kicked in.

"Whoa there!" the deep voice soothed. "It's just me."

And then her heart stopped completely when she found herself looking into the sleepy face of Cam. It took her back to that dance. She pushed the memory away.

"Sorry, I didn't think anyone was awake yet," Grace said, rubbing the sleep out of her eyes.

"Just me. My mattress was killing me. I think I'll have to switch it with Jake's when he's not looking," he muttered, rubbing his face in his hands.

"Aren't there other ones in the cabin?" Grace's eyebrows scrunched together. There were only three men in a cabin with room for eight, assuming it had the identical setup to the women's cabin.

"Yes, but that wouldn't be as fun," he said with a devil-ish smile.

"Trouble," she stated. "And you look so innocent."

Happy to get a relaxed and normal reaction from her, he chuckled.

Sniffing the air as they walked toward the kitchen, he said, "I believe you owe me a coffee."

"Well, it just so happens that I have brewed a pot. Or most of a pot. That thing is huge. It may take all morning to finish brewing. Let me get you a cup."

Grace reached into the cupboard with the mugs she had found on her earlier search and grabbed a couple: one slightly uneven but beautiful brown pottery mug and another that said "Don't pee upwind" with a picture of a cartoon moose holding up his finger to gauge the direction of the wind. Holding the mug out for him to read, she said, "A good reminder for you."

Reading it brought out a burst of laughter.

Her heart jumped in her throat at the sight of his dazzling smile combined with his general hunky-ness. Quickly turning toward the fridge to gather her wits, Grace asked, "What do you take in it?"

"Cream and sugar."

Grace fixed the coffees, and they toasted each other before taking a sip. Forcing down her sip of the bitter coffee, she looked up to see Cam's eyes bulging from its strength. Holding up a finger to indicate "just a second," she started moving toward the tea kettle.

"No, it's fine." Cam laughed. Nodding toward the door, he asked, "Want to head outside so we don't wake anyone up?"

Grace happily made her way toward the entrance, careful not to spill her coffee. Walking behind, he reached over her shoulder to push open the door, and the springs creaked loudly in protest.

He shut the door as silently as possible and, grabbing her hand, pulled her toward the dock. "Have a seat," he said when they arrived at her chair. "Here, hold my cup while I get another chair."

"Sure."

Her heart thrilled with happiness. It was so easy being around Cam. But unfamiliar too. Grace wondered what Psycho Cop would do if he saw this. *No,* she told herself. *I don't want to know.*

Cam returned with a chair for himself and turned it inward a little so they could see the water and visit comfortably at the same time.

"Okay, so, I wanted to have a chance to talk to you myself before Mr. Camping-Trip-Organizer-Guy got up and started bossing us around," he began. "First of all, I wanted to say thanks for sharing last night. We all knew something huge was going on with you, but we didn't want to pry."

"Thanks. Not sure you all needed to know that, though."

"No, maybe not, but I'm glad I do." He paused, elbows on knees.

She looked at him.

"Why?" Grace asked, feeling hopeful, stupid, needy, and terrible all at the same time. She'd just escaped from a madman and was broken. She would just mess up the life of anyone she got close to right now.

72

"Well, I don't know if you remember me." He paused, rubbing the back of his neck. "But I have not forgotten you."

Suddenly she was unable to hear with the sound of her heart banging in her chest. *He remembered.* And it sounded like maybe he remembered it the same way: unbelievably romantic, instant and intense physical attraction, and terribly bittersweet—when she told him she was seeing someone, they had known it couldn't go anywhere. Not knowing how to express all that, she simply said, "I remember." Grace carefully looked him in the eyes to try to communicate how much it had hurt to walk away from him that night.

He didn't say anything. Pulling in, then slowly releasing a deep breath, he dropped his head and swallowed hard. With a pained expression and a shake of his head, he asked, "How can a dance or two and so little time together make such an impression?"

"I don't know. And how do you explain that to someone? Meeting random people happens all the time. But it doesn't happen like that very often. Not for me, anyway." She timidly looked at him from the corner of his eye.

"Or me."

Again, silence. Comfortable silence.

A loon trilled from somewhere on the water.

"So, what happened after that?" Cam asked. "Was this the guy you were with?" To her nod, he continued, "You went home, and things were good for a while?"

Looking out at the water, she said, "They weren't great, but in my mind, I'd committed to the relationship. I knew he was jealous and didn't dare tell him I had been to the bar. I made my friend promise to say we'd gone for supper."

"Did he believe you?"

"No. Actually, he questioned me as to why he didn't see any charges come out of the bank account."

"Seriously?"

"Yes. That was his thing. Control. Keeping tabs. He was so insecure, or maybe he just liked keeping me 'in my place.' I had to say that my friend had bought dinner to say thanks for the visit, and he must have thought that sounded reasonable. But I haven't been able to visit her again, and she's been my best friend since grade school."

"I wish I had made you take my number or even my name. It may have given you an out a little sooner," Cam said quietly.

"You asked me my name, my first name anyway, but I made a conscious decision not to ask for yours. I didn't want to have that to hold on to. I knew I was in trouble." Grace smiled sheepishly.

His eyes flashed in happiness as he gave her a wide grin, taking her breath away. Reacting to the intensity of emotions, she suddenly felt overwhelmed. "I can't believe I am talking to you. I can't believe we are having this conversation." Grace jumped up and walked to the end of the dock overlooking the water.

Standing, Cam took a few steps toward her. Rubbing the stubble on his chin, he stood at her side. "It feels good, no?" Lowering his voice, he asked, "Are you worried about your ex?"

She turned to face him. "Yes, I'm worried about whether he will let me *be* his ex—a living ex, that is." Grace shrugged. "He is looking for me, and if I don't come back, I do believe he will find a clean and simple way of getting rid of me."

"We will help you," he promised, grabbing her hand.

"He has no conscience." She stared at him. "He will kill you too."

"Good morning!" Cody called as he stepped onto the dock behind them.

They both cried out and nearly jumped up out of their skin.

"What the—" Cam said, too stunned to finish.

The gape on Cody's face stopped them in their tracks, and the anger Grace had felt at being frightened turned into a burst of laughter.

"Okay, remind me to never interrupt your conversation when you have a canoe paddle in your hand, an axe, or"— he looked at the cups in their hands—"a full cup of coffee for that matter." Turning away, he added, "Maybe you shouldn't make the coffee quite so strong next time."

As Cody walked away, shaking his head and muttering something about getting chummy, the breakfast bell rang.

Back at the lodge, the group was in various stages of dress and alertness. Jim and Evelyn were walking back to the dining table with a bowl of fruit and granola in one hand and a glass of juice and a croissant in the other. Grace's stomach grumbled.

"After you," Cam offered as Nicki came out of the bathroom and jumped in line behind her.

"I haven't slept that good in years!" she said, contentedly running her fingers through her curly hair.

As Jake and Kat came shuffling into the room, she murmured in sleepy agreement.

"Eat up!" Louis opened a container of muffins. "Banana bread and bran."

"Cam, grab a bran muffin for me," Jim called from the table. "Traveling always stops me up," he said more to himself as he ate a spoonful of yogurt and granola.

"Jim!" Evelyn shrieked. He only shrugged, and she waved him off. "Anyway, did you sleep well, Margot?"

Sitting down across from her, Margot replied, "Well, I probably would have had I rolled over instead of getting up to catch the northern lights. I hope I didn't disturb you."

"Not me," Evelyn replied. "I slept like the dead without Jim's snoring in my ear."

"Instead, he kept *me* up," Jake said in monotone from the end of the table. He yawned with his eyes closed, his shiny black hair sticking out every which way. "And that's why I look like this."

Kat stood behind him and smiled. "You look even sexier when you're sleepy." She ruffled his hair, threw her arms over his shoulders, and leaning in, hugged him from behind. She put her chin on his shoulder before giving him a little kiss on the cheek.

"How about we get a tent for tonight?" Kat suggested, looking at Jake.

He nodded, eyes still closed.

"Uh, where do you plan on setting up?" Margot asked.

Louis smiled. "There's a little camping area on the other side of the campfire. It's far enough away that the smoke won't bother you."

Cody chuckled. "And far enough away that those of us single and looking don't need to be reminded of our unfortunate situations." His eyes slid to Grace.

Grace looked down at her food but not before noticing Cam staring at Cody in disbelief.

Smoothing over the moment, as always, Louis jumped in.

"Take your time with breakfast. Cody and I will start washing up so we can get an early start. Please meet up at the dock at nine o'clock with your art supplies for the day, whether it be a paintbrush and canvas, a camera, or a journal. Cam, you and I will practice the art of fishing. Don't worry, I am not the least bit creative either, man."

"Sounds great."

Not to be outdone, Cody jumped in with the last word. "Oh, and make sure you fill a water bottle for yourself for the day. You can find them on the island in the kitchen. They are numbered, so remember which is yours. It'll be yours for the duration of your trip."

CHAPTER 7

Under Our Feet as Well as Over Our Heads

—Henry David Thoreau

THEY STOOD IN BRIGHT ORANGE LIFEJACKETS WAITING for instruction and smelling of bug spray and sunscreen. Grace pulled her cap on tight and threw her much lighter knapsack over both shoulders in the hopes that she wouldn't drop it in the water when it was time to get into the canoe.

"Okay, we have five teams and we're going to mix it up. Just because you are married—or part of a couple—doesn't mean you should canoe together. In fact, because you are married, or part of a couple, it is a very good idea *not* to canoe together," Louis teased. "The team names are Chickadee, Eagle, Hawk, Kingfisher, and Loon. Grace and I will be Chickadee, Cam and Margot are Eagle, Jake and Evelyn are Hawk, Jim and Kat are the Kingfisher boat, and . . . Nicki and Cody will be Loon. I tried to match it by personality," Louis said, deadpan. "As you may have noticed, the team names are on the bow of each canoe, so you can leave your belongings in yours and they won't get mixed up."

Moving over to their respective canoes, Grace felt a whoosh of relief. It would be easy to spend the day in a canoe with Louis. He was quiet and knowledgeable and would be comfortable with silence. In the rickety, old boathouse, they each took an end of the canoe and carefully lifted it up an inch or two before sliding it out of its rack.

"Do you want to put it overhead?" Grace asked.

"Sure," Louis replied.

Knowing he was experienced, she didn't hesitate. It would be less awkward than carrying the bulky canoe at their knees.

"Ready . . . up!" she called and followed Louis's lead to be sure their timing was right.

Once the canoe was up over their heads, she shouted, "Ready, split!" hoping he would know what she was talking about. The rowing lingo was ingrained in her, but she wasn't sure it applied to canoeing.

"To the shoulders?" he called back.

"Yep," she quickly replied before the weight of the canoe became too uncomfortable.

Louis settled it on his left shoulder, Grace put it on her right.

"Show-offs!" Nicki called good-naturedly as they walked down toward the water.

"Why don't you sit at the front of the boat? I can steer if you like," Louis suggested.

"Sure thing."

Easy-peasy, Grace thought. It would feel good to get on the water again. Being on a body of water was second nature to her now; she'd rowed on rivers, lakes, and canals, large and small. Even though the canoeing stroke would be different than pulling an oar, the way the water would slow the paddle would be familiar. Grace knew the need to balance the boat while working with a teammate to make the most efficient use of their energy, and through precise timing and similar form, propel the boat forward. She couldn't wait to give it a try.

As a rower, one becomes intimately in tune to the various types of water: calm water, water with a current, and water affected by gusts of wind. Rowers immediately adapt their thinking to how they will pull the oar through the water. Can they put it in crisply and focus on the pull? Or do they have to be extra sharp in their entry and really quick at the finish so their blade doesn't get pulled under by the current and capsize the boat? If the wind is blowing from the side, the rower may need to lean into it a little to keep the boat balanced. Not great for the back, but subtle shifts in the body posture make for a more efficient row.

Today was a beautiful, calm morning, so Grace wouldn't have to do more than figure out the best way to sit in the canoe and practice getting the paddle in and out in long, smooth strokes. Once they got to the middle of the lake, Louis said to hold up until the others joined them. "We're going to give a little demo on the basics of paddling," he explained. Once the rest had caught up and some instruction was given, she was able to start practicing this new skill with confidence.

The destination today was west via a corridor with cliffs on either side. They paddled through some marshy areas, but there was only one portage, thankfully, as it was a little tricky. It was tough walking with a canoe overhead, light as they were, with blood rushing away from their hands and arms. Some went back to help others, and the party made it through without too much trouble.

Grace was happy to get her body moving again. She had started to feel restless and stiff and needed to work through some nerves. She imagined *he* was searching for her with cold calculation. Knowing he wouldn't rest until he'd found her, he would be up all night scouring his sources, contacting his friends for help (and hers to see what they knew), and keeping his anger boiling just under the surface until he was able to unleash it on her.

He might even call her dad to feel him out.

Shoot. Dad. I need to let him know I'm okay.

The frantic thought sped up her stroke rate. Grace realized that Louis hadn't been able to adjust to the new, unexpected speed when the canoe suddenly veered to the left. She forced herself to slow down and concentrate on the repetition of the stroke in order to calm down again. After a few minutes, Louis and Grace found themselves ahead of the others and pulled sideways to wait for them to catch up.

As the ripples on the water subsided, Grace turned in her seat so she could speak to Louis. "Can I ask a favor?"

"Sure, what can I do?" He set his paddle across his lap and waited.

"Well, you know a little about what's happening in my life right now." To his nod, she continued, "I am wondering if you have a way to contact a friend of yours. A trustworthy one who might be willing to send my dad an email. Just to let him know I'm okay."

"Sure, I could do that." Louis gave a brief nod.

"I wouldn't want to put them in any danger. I wonder if there's a way they could do it from a remote location—that is, not at their home and not with their personal email. Maybe they could set up a new one."

"This guy means business," he said, holding Grace with a steady gaze.

"Yeah, he's scary. The thing is, if you met him, you'd think he's a great guy."

"Hm. Maybe." He paused. "I'd like to think I'd sense the real him somehow. It's one of my many talents." Grace smiled as he puffed out his chest a little.

Nodding, she could believe that Louis would be more in tune with the nuances of people than the average person.

"Oh, and, sorry, I am being a bit paranoid on this, but maybe this friend of yours shouldn't be any relation to you or connected to the camp in any way."

"Absolutely. Just leave it to me." He gave a small smile, then turned toward the approaching canoes.

"Thanks," Grace said as Nicki and Cody came sliding to a stop beside them.

They paddled for another hour, exiting the lake through a narrow channel that opened into a larger body of water before reaching their "outdoor destination for creative inspiration," as Cody had dubbed it. It was an island with a beautiful rocky shoreline, which they were able to access via a swampy area. The bottom came up to greet them as they glided onto shore. One by one, they stepped out of their canoes and tied off the boats to the nearby trees. A little tired and low on fuel, they trudged down a narrow, worn trail that emerged into a clearing.

They stopped when they heard a scream.

Grace quickly stepped to the side while Louis and Jake went running back down the trail; it had sounded like Kat.

Those left behind froze, wondering what had happened, and strained to hear anything they could. Shortly after, there was some chuckling and complaining in a voice a little higher than the others' as they emerged from the trail. Cody, Louis, Jake, and Kat came out with three smiles and a frown.

"Leech," Cody explained.

A shiver went down Grace's spine thinking about having to get back into the canoe later today.

Gathering in the clearing, they looked back out over the lake from which they had come. The land sat a few feet above the water, giving the impression that the view was made for them. The trees, thick in the distance, came right to the water's edge, the randomness of them fascinating. The water lay flat beneath them and reflected their image, doubling their beauty, as once was not enough. A small island sat between them and the far shore, providing a resting spot for migrating birds.

As Cody tossed out bags of nuts and chocolate, he announced, "You have some time to find a location for your artistic endeavors for the day. There are lots of little paths around the island to explore that will take you to various private areas. Find your spot and get started, but make your way back for lunch when you hear the bell."

Louis held a large cowbell in his hands and gave it a few deep rings in demonstration.

"As you know, Cam is pursuing the art of fishing this week, so he'll be catching our lunch today. Hopefully he has some talent, or we may go hungry." Cody let out a hearty laugh. "We'll have a shore lunch once everything is all cooked up, then you can head back and continue working."

"Don't worry, I saw them pack some salami in case the fish aren't biting," Cam said with a wry smile, picking up his tackle box and making his way toward the shore.

Grace had brought along her journal and cell phone to take pictures. Writing a little and taking pictures would be the extent of her creativity for the day. She reached into her backpack to pull out her phone and hoped she would be able to capture some of the beauty with the built-in camera. Grace had always found, however, that no matter how successful the shot was at forever holding that moment in time, it was never as good as being there. Pictures can't capture the crisp air, the musty scent of the boreal forest, the sun on your face, or the gentle breeze. It could only be imagined. But it was the best a person could do to hold on to the moment until they survived another winter and returned again the next year. Unable to find the phone in her pack, she decided to leave it until she found a spot where she could pull everything out.

Margot was at the edge of the clearing, already taking pictures of the water. Nicki was hiking down one trail with her tote bag full of paint, brushes, small canvases, and other tools for her craft. Jake and Kat went hand in hand down a trail more off the beaten path. He had his guitar, she her notebook. Jim and Evelyn stood chatting, apparently trying to decide what they were going to do. Grace wondered what they had planned for the rest of the day, as she hadn't gotten a sense of what they were hoping to get from their time here this week. They didn't seem overtly artistic, but hey, Grace knew better than to judge a book by its cover.

Wandering along a path that ran deeper into the trees, she looked for some privacy and a place to write, not necessarily with a view. The path took a natural bend that led around a corner. Those were the paths she found hard to resist—those paths that keep you walking just to see what could be there. Usually, there isn't much, except more of the same, but it's the excitement of the unknown that keeps you going down that path.

The breathing and natural rhythm and flow of her body as it moved was cathartic in itself and added to the joy of the moment. There had been other moments like this already. Like watching a campfire flame flicker or clouds move slowly through the sky. They are the moments when you get to put your mind in neutral and just be.

Grace hadn't had a chance to do that lately. When she was a kid, she probably did it every day. In church, at the dinner table, in school, or in the backyard. There was never any rush. So she sat down on a large, flat rock and decided to just sit for a while. She gazed out into the distance across the water and watched the light twinkle like diamonds off the ripples. A breath of wind blew her hair and cleared her mind. After a few minutes, Grace opened her journal, pulled out a pen, and wrote the first words that came to mind.

Silence.

Stillness.

Peace.

Freedom to be. To be me.

Hidden.

Safe.

The words weren't going to win her a poetry contest, but it didn't matter. They were *her* words. It was the act of writing, of getting the words out of her head that had always helped Grace to come to terms with what was going on in her life.

Knowing she had nowhere to be, Grace sat on the ground, crossed her legs, and closed her eyes. She tried to clear her mind as she had been encouraged to do in yoga classes, without success in the past. Maybe here she could. She breathed in and out, in and out, and let time pass without acknowledging it or worrying about getting something done.

Hearing the cowbell in the distance, Grace opened her eyes. She left her pack where it was and headed back up the path to the clearing.

Louis knelt on the ground and held an old hand towel around the handle of a large, black wrought iron skillet. The heat from the fire made the lard sizzle as it cooked the battered fish. He used tongs to flip a piece of fish; the other side was a lovely golden brown.

Evelyn craned her neck toward the pan from where she stood. "That's cooking up nicely."

Cody stirred bite-size potatoes and finely chopped onions and peppers in an aluminum steel pan that sat over a small propane burner. They were doused in butter and covered in spices. He lifted the serving spoon out for a moment and called, "Come and get it!"

"The paper plates and forks are right there." He pointed to where they sat on a red-and-white checkered tablecloth that had been laid on the ground. "And just past Louis, you'll find some seasoning salt and lemon pepper if you want to spice up your fish."

Jake grabbed the first plate and got things started. "What kind of fish did you catch?"

Louis grabbed a large fillet and set it on Jake's plate. "This here is walleye, also known as pickerel." Pointing to a tub of raw fish, he said, "That there is jackfish, or northern pike."

"Is there a difference between the two?" Jake picked up the fish and took a bite.

"Whoa, that's still hot!" Louis laughed as Jake covered his open mouth with his hand and waited for it to cool down.

Cam chuckled as he set a freshly washed filleting knife and board beside the base of a nearby tree. "The walleye's a nicer fish. The flesh is firm and white."

Jake nodded, blowing on the walleye before risking another bite. He stepped back as Kat, Margot, and Nicki filled their plates and waited to get some fish.

"That's how a lot of people feel." There was a loud hiss as Louis added more lard to his pan. "The northern pike is slimy, so it turns some people off, but I would say it's the best-tasting fish anywhere." He reached for the bucket of fish and dragged it closer. "Let's get some of that pike cooking so you can try it." The pan hissed and spit as he threw the fillets into the skillet.

The smell of cooked potatoes and fish made Grace's stomach growl, signaling that it was time to get in line. The potatoes steamed as Cody scooped them onto her plate. Louis gave her two small pieces of walleye. "Don't forget to come back to try this other one." He tapped his tongs on the fillets still cooking in his pan. "They're not ready quite yet."

"I'll be back," Grace assured him with a nod.

They filled their bellies and threw their paper plates into the fire.

"I'll take your forks and wash them up when we get back to the lodge." Cody walked around to collect them.

"Make sure to grab some chocolate before you go." Louis broke large chocolate bars into small pieces before opening them and making a plate out of the wrapper.

Grace grabbed a large piece of chocolate, thanked them for lunch, and made her way back to her spot.

Once there, she picked up her pen and journal and ambled over to a large yellow birch tree. Turning, she leaned back against it and slid down its smooth bark to sit on the ground. Legs stretched out in front of her, she crossed her ankles, opened the journal, and held it on her lap. She groaned at her full belly and wished she could have a nap. Looking at the blank sheet of paper, she thought about what she wanted to say. *What message do I want to share with the world?* Tapping her foot, she put the tip of the pen in her mouth. *How am I supposed to share any words of wisdom when I don't even know who I am anymore?*

She wrote anyway.

Who am I?

Who am I now?

Who was I then?

Certainly not the same person.

She loved who she was growing up. Her parents had loved her unconditionally and applauded all that she was. With that support, she was happy, confident, sure that she was going to be an asset to this world.

Over the last few years, Grace had been told that her instincts were wrong, that she was selfish and that she should do more. But not that, or that. This. Do this, and if you don't . . . the threat was always left hanging.

She knew it was wrong. She knew he was manipulating her. He knew Grace was made to please and avoid confrontation, and she knew these personality traits weren't bad with the right person, the right man. Well, that wouldn't happen again. She would never get herself into a situation like that again.

Grace leaned her head back against the tree. A breeze blew across her forehead, and she tried to hold on to the comfort it brought. The movement of a bird overhead caught her eye and, as her head was tilted skyward, she noticed the tree trunk. She studied the tree from that angle, the distinctive trunk of the birch tree reaching upward, the top barely visible from her vantage point. It appeared to be stretching to the heavens with a purpose. *What would a tree's purpose be?* Grace chuckled to herself. *Maybe the same as the rest of us. Maybe the tree also asks itself: Why am I here? What is my life's purpose?*

Inspired, Grace wanted to capture the moment with a picture. She would name it *Looking to Heaven for Help.* Standing, she thought she might also take a picture in every direction around herself, pivoting a little to her right each time she snapped. *That would be so cool*, she thought, imagining it. *What would it represent? A moment in time? My hiding spot?* Whatever it was, she knew it would be one of those moments that would be forever etched in her mind. The start of a new life. A turning point. *A Turning Point.* That's exactly what she would call these images were she to print, frame, and hang them somewhere.

Thinking about this new life and where it would take her, Grace bent to pick up her knapsack to get her phone so she could take the pictures. She reached into the main compartment again and couldn't feel the cool, hard lump she was looking for. Dumping the contents onto the ground, she rummaged through her things but couldn't find it. She opened the small zipper on the top, then the bigger pouch on the front. Her phone wasn't there.

And with a feeling as sudden as it was intense, she felt a wave of nausea. Where was her phone? As Grace stood, her head spinning, she felt like she'd been punched in the stomach. Panicked, she went through all the places she could have left it. She hadn't used it since she'd been at Thompson Lake. *I haven't used it since I was at Thompson Lake!* And with that realization, she pictured it exactly where she had left it. On the bedside table of the Tulip Room. Hyperventilating, Grace squeezed her eyes shut and gasped to control her breath. She spun around in all directions, making sure there was no reason for the terror she was feeling. It was only a phone. *You don't need the phone*, she told herself. But it wasn't the phone—it was *him*. He still had a hold on her even though he was not physically there.

Her heart continued to race, and her breathing came fast. Grace leaned over, holding her knees. *He isn't here. He isn't here. He isn't even close to here.* Grace forced herself to slowly breathe. In. Out. She stood still. In silence. Everything would be okay. Everything will be fine. Someday.

Rattled, Grace stuffed everything back into her pack and started walking back to the meeting point. She needed to move, to get away from this particular spot now that it was no longer a refuge. *Get it together, Grace,* she told herself. What was that phrase her friend used to say back in school? "Bon Courage." It wished the individual to have both courage and good luck. Grace had always loved that phrase. She would need a bit of both in the days and weeks to come.

No one was at the clearing when she arrived, so she settled herself at the edge where the land fell away to the water and dangled her legs over the side. She sat there until her heart rate had slowed and the panic had fully subsided. The water was so beautiful and inviting. Grace swung her legs to the side, kicked off her sneakers, and pulled off her sweatshirt. She had worn her bikini and swim shorts in case the opportunity to go for a dip presented itself and, wanting to act for once instead of thinking through all the pros and cons like she normally would, Grace scrambled to her feet, stepped back, and took a running jump. Arms overhead, she squealed as she flew through the air.

The shock of the cold water quickly changed to refreshment as she popped back to the surface and warmed herself by treading water. Grace couldn't control her grin—the water felt so good, so nice and cool. Grace floated on her back, basking in the freedom of her impulsive decision. She took a few strokes and swam a little farther offshore and stopped when she got tired to float on her back some more. Grace looked down at the black water beneath her and realized she couldn't see the bottom. She wondered how deep it was and what was down there. Was there a little fish just waiting to take a nibble on her toe? Looking back up at the shoreline from where she'd jumped, she realized she wasn't sure how she would get back out of the water. The embankment was only three to four feet high but just high enough to make it impossible to reach the top. She probably should have thought of that before she jumped in.

She swam back toward the shore and called to anyone within earshot, "Uh, hey, guys? Hello? A little help over here . . . ?" There was no answer.

She saw the marshy area off to the left of the cliff, which wasn't overly appealing, thinking back to that leech that had been on Kat's ankle. Just the thought of coming out of the water covered in leeches made her skin crawl. The stuff of nightmares. She would rather tread water all afternoon. The embankment went off to the right as far as she could see. Beyond that, the large island ended, but whether there was shore around that corner that she could easily climb up, Grace wasn't certain. It would be a long way to swim to find herself in the same spot farther away from camp.

Bon Courage, she repeated to herself.

Grace shivered. The adrenaline from her panic attack long gone, Grace found her energy was low after the long canoe trip this morning. Shoot. The one time she decided to live on the edge and not worry about every little thing . . . It's just that the cliff didn't seem that bad from the top. It was only four feet, at most. With no hand or footholds to use to climb back up.

Someone will come back soon, she thought. Grace floated on her back, trying to push away the newly arising unease and save some energy. Giving herself a pep talk, Grace reminded herself that her body was capable of doing much more than she thought it could. She had learned that with rowing. Who would have thought she'd be able to row for six hours in one day? But she had done it a few years back in a forty-one-mile rowing trek down the Ottawa River from Ottawa to Montebello, Quebec. If she could do that, she could do this. Tread water, float. Tread water, float.

Her teeth started chattering. *Where is everyone?* There was a small island in the middle of the lake that looked to be within yelling range and, more importantly, climbable. Deciding it was time to head for land, Grace started for the island with a side stroke. Really, it was the only stroke she could do comfortably since she didn't like putting her face in the water. The backstroke was an option as well, but she never seemed to make any headway with it.

The longer Grace swam, the farther away the island appeared, but with no other options, she kept moving toward it, one stroke at a time. *I think I can, I think I can.* Pure determination. That's what it took to get up at 4:45 every morning to make it down to the boathouse for practice. One stroke after the next. Repeat. She went into the zone and just kept going. Eventually, Grace reached the island and was able to put her feet on solid ground.

The island was maybe sixty feet by one hundred with a few spruce trees providing some shelter from the wind and sun. It contained lots of the flat rock of the Canadian Shield and, away from the trees, Grace lay down on one in an attempt to dry off and get some warmth back in her bones. She dozed off for a few minutes and woke to the sound of a loon yodeling a little offshore. The sound did much to calm her soul, and she smiled to herself. Grace loved the feeling of being physically exhausted. The stress just slipped away with the released endorphins, leaving such a wonderful feeling.

More alert now, Grace looked back across the water toward camp and still saw no movement.

Tucking one leg under, she rolled to the side and pushed herself up. After stretching an arm across her body, Grace began to stroll around the little island. Roots poked through patches of hard earth and lush moss—in the perfect shade of green—that covered the ground in all the nooks and crannies where water had gathered. Near the end of the island, the ground sloped more naturally toward the water, making it an ideal place to pull up a canoe. Her eye caught some disturbed ground, and she realized that someone else had thought the same thing not long ago.

Eyeing the markings in the dried mud, Grace wondered when the footprints had been made. Looking across the water, she tried to determine which direction the lodge was from there. Was this a main route? She didn't think it could be after the portage and all the small, serene lakes they'd passed through this morning.

She needed to get back to the group.

Turning to head back to the south shore from which she came, something caught her eye. Moss hanging loosely from a join in the tree looked a little out of place. On closer inspection, Grace saw that it wasn't attached, and as she went to move it, the corner of a black plastic box was revealed. *What is that?* she thought. Realization dawned just as Grace questioned what she was seeing. No, it wasn't a camper's forgotten first aid kit. *This must be one of those geocaches they had been talking about last night at happy hour.* Cautiously, she reached up and removed the box from its hiding place.

CHAPTER 8

Be His Friend

—Henry David Thoreau

*H*OW DO YOU OPEN THIS THING? GRACE TURNED THE BOX over in her hands. Pushing along a line near the top and using a bit of pressure, she popped it open. Carefully lifting the lid so that nothing would fall out, she found a small Ziploc bag inside. Inside the bag was a piece of paper folded into a square. Opening the bag and unfolding the paper, Grace saw a line or two of writing with quotes at the beginning and end. Turning it over, she saw that it had been signed "Xander."

"Hello!"

Grace jumped. A silver canoe with two male paddlers slid onto shore. Heart pounding and still holding her newfound treasures, Grace stood tall, muscles taut as they stepped out of the canoe. One was tall and skinny and walked toward her with a swagger and a smug look. The other was shorter and stockier and was pulling his jeans back up into place after dragging the canoe farther out of the water.

Looking around, the first saw that she was alone, then noticed the box in her hand. "Trying your hand at treasure hunting?" He nodded with his chin at the box.

"I guess so," she replied, looking down at the box and paper in her hand. "Quite accidentally, I assure you." Grace laughed awkwardly. "I jumped in the lake without a paddle and ended up here."

He smiled, showing his crooked, yellow teeth. "I'm Sebastian," he said, extending a cold, long-fingered hand.

Grace hesitated before accepting the handshake. He was friendly, but there was an underlying . . . menace.

"Marc." The other, bigger guy waved while securing the canoe.

"So, what did you find?" Sebastian had an intensity in his eyes that went beyond mild curiosity. Grace looked down to read it just as he held out his hand and waited for her to pass him the paper.

Frowning, she gave it to him.

Marc walked up beside Sebastian, and the two read the note together. Looking at each other for a moment, Sebastian pursed his lips before Marc stepped away, hand on the back of his neck.

"What is it?" Grace asked, looking from one to the other.

Ignoring her, Sebastian said to Marc, "He shouldn't have come up here alone. Anything could happen. Cell coverage is spotty. You can't count on it."

"What did he put in the box?" Marc glanced at Grace's hand.

"Oh, I didn't have a chance to look yet." She noticed the little plastic Ziploc bag contained two small pills with happy faces on them. Grace held it up for them to see, feeling uncomfortable. She had no idea what it was and wasn't sure she wanted to find out.

"Awesome!" Marc grinned. "This trip just got fun."

"That's Xander for you. Lucky for him it wasn't a conservation officer who found it." Sebastian smirked. "It's gotta be him. There can't be too many Xanders up here."

Grace passed them the box and the baggie and held out her hand for the note. It read, "Two—" She looked up. "It starts with a two. Is this the second note?" To their nods, Grace asked, "Really? What did the first one say?" forgetting she hadn't even read the second note yet.

Sebastian pulled it out of his back pocket and passed it to her.

"1 — I went to the woods because I wished to live deliberately, to front only the essential facts of life and see if I could not learn what it had to teach, and not, when I came to die, discover that I had not lived."

—Henry David Thoreau

"Flip it over," Sebastian urged.

Hey, guys. I knew I'd get you here one way or another. Come and find me!

—Xander.

Coordinates: 45.6592 N, 78.6900 W

"These coordinates, is this where we are?" Grace asked Sebastian.

Again, he nodded.

Grace read the second note, the one she had found, next.

"2 — If a man does not keep pace with his companions, perhaps it is because he hears a different drummer. Let him step to the music which he hears, however measured or far away."

—Henry David Thoreau

Another Thoreau quote. She turned it over.

I definitely hear a different drummer. He led me here.

—Xander.

Coordinates: 45.4263 N, 78.3569W

Grace passed the papers back. "Looks like you have an adventure ahead. You're trying to find this guy?"

"Yeah, Xander, Alexander Fortin, is a good buddy of ours, and he's been missing for a while," Marc said, voice deepening.

"How long?" Grace asked.

"He was due back a few weeks ago. Didn't realize he hadn't gotten home for almost a week. Just figured he was busy getting settled in. Once we heard he hadn't gotten back, we weren't too worried. As he said, he marches to his own drum." Sebastian shrugged.

"It was maybe another week before we started to think something could have happened, then till we got orga-nized . . ." Marc trailed off. "I'm not sure we'll find him in time if he's in trouble."

"Did you get in touch with the police?" Grace asked.

"Yeah, I gave them a call," Sebastian answered briefly. "They said they would get on it."

Speaking of police, Grace asked, "Did he leave some-thing in the first box?"

"Yes, but it was a lot milder than this," Sebastian said, looking at the bag in his hand.

"We slept like babies after, but boy was I hungry!" Marc laughed at his own joke.

Eyes widening, Grace glanced across the water, then changed the subject. "I went for a swim off that island over there and couldn't get back up the incline."

"Over there?" Marc asked incredulously. "You swam from there?"

"Yeah," she admitted. "Not the smartest move. Can you guys give me a lift back?"

Letting out a long exhale, Sebastian looked down at her and said, "Sure, we've got to find a place to camp tonight, and this little island is not going to cut it. Let's go."

They jumped in the canoe and made the short trek to the other island.

Nicki waved to them from shore as their canoe approached. Kat jumped and hollered. Jake rang the cowbell. Cam stood stiffly beside Cody, not saying a word. *Whatever*, Grace thought.

"Rule number one was, Miss Grace?" Cody admonished as they approached the shore.

"Don't swim alone," Grace recited with an edge in her voice. Annoyed with herself and not wanting a lecture, she stepped out of the canoe and marched away from the boat to find her pack and water bottle. Tipping it back, she gulped the water down.

As Louis helped pull the boat up from the marshy water, Cam scrutinized Marc and Sebastian.

Cody, ever the spokesperson, offered, "Thanks for bringing Grace back. Doing a little canoe camping, are you?"

"Looking for a buddy, actually," Sebastian replied as they made their way up the path. "You haven't seen a guy our age traveling on his own, have you?"

"Recently?" Louis asked.

"About a month ago," Marc shook his head. "He let Sebastian know he was coming up here but when we didn't hear from him for a couple of weeks, we stopped by his place. There were a lot of fliers in his mailbox, so we knew he hadn't been home in a while." Marc stood with his hands on his hips. "I called a couple of his friends, but no one had heard from him and no one had even known he was going camping, so we figured we'd better see if he was up here hurt or something," Marc explained. "Sebastian let the police know that he was missing and where he had gone, but we thought we'd come looking too."

"It would be the OPP, the Ontario Provincial Police, that would do the investigation up here," Jim said, tipping his head from side to side. "Have they been around?"

"No." Cody glanced at Louis for confirmation. "We haven't seen anyone who isn't from around these parts by themselves. It's not really a good idea to travel on your own. Does he know what he's doing?"

"Xander is a pretty bright guy, and he used to camp with his dad up here a lot when he was a kid," Sebastian replied.

"Still doesn't make it a good idea. All you've got to do is lose your footing and you've broken your leg. A broken leg makes it tough to portage," Louis retorted.

"Yeah, yeah. Look. It wasn't my idea," Sebastian grumbled.

"Speaking of portaging . . ." Louis began, eyes focused in the distance at the dark, shape-shifting clouds moving quickly across the sky. "That sky doesn't look so good. I'm not sure that we should be heading back to the lodge tonight."

"Lodge . . ." Sebastian said, eyes narrowing. "Is that the one on White Spruce Road?"

"The very same." Louis nodded.

Grace stepped into her sneakers, then kneeled down to tie the laces. Cam reached for his fishing rod, then slung his pack over his shoulder. Grace assumed he was taking his things down to the canoes, so when she stood and found that he had stopped mid-step, she wondered what he was doing. His focus was on Sebastian, who was eyeing Grace with appreciation. Biting her lip, she realized she was wearing only a bikini top and swim shorts. Embarrassed, Grace kept her head down as Cam marched to the path that led to the leech-filled waters. *He* wouldn't have approved of her wearing a swimsuit in front of all these people, either.

Grace pulled out a sweatshirt from her pack and put it on. Was it really because of what she was wearing? Well, if it was, he could suck a lemon—*no one* was going to tell her what to wear anymore. Maybe it wasn't that, anyway. Could be he just didn't care for Sebastian and Marc. Or that she'd brought them here. Regardless, what Cam thought about anything wasn't really her concern.

A rough log bench had been placed next to the fire. Grace settled herself on it and reached out to warm her hands. Louis gave her a blanket, and she wrapped it around her legs. Margot brought over a cup with peppermint and licorice tea, explaining that it was good for digestion and relaxing muscles. "We had just been brewing some when we saw you coming."

As she took a sip of the tea, Cody handed her some chocolate. Grace thanked him and gobbled it down, knowing she needed some sugar to help with the dizziness that she had been experiencing. She often felt dizzy after a morning row if she didn't get a chance to eat soon enough.

Cody offered some chocolate to the others. "I don't like the look of that sky, either, Louis. We had better get started on a shelter for the night—and quick."

Grace looked up and out over the water back the way they had come earlier in the day. It was startling to see how the sky went from blue and sunny with full white clouds overhead to a bank of jet-black clouds in the distance. The dark clouds, flashing with lightning, released a sheet of rain that was moving rapidly over the water toward them.

"But we don't have any tents," Grace said.

"Survival 101, I'm afraid." Louis smiled reassuringly as he walked away to get preparations started.

"Shoot. I'm sorry if I delayed things." Grace shivered as a cool breeze blew through the site. At the same moment, a wolf howled in the distance, raising goose bumps on her skin.

"No, no," Cody consoled. "We've only been back about half an hour and wouldn't have gotten away any earlier," he said, glancing at his watch. "Right, Louis?"

"Yes, that's right. Not to worry, Grace." Louis was efficiently packing up his supplies.

The wind picked up just then, and Cody waved for Jake to follow him as he jogged in the direction of where they had left the canoes. He called back to Sebastian and Marc over his shoulder. "You boys might want to pull your canoe farther up on shore and tie it up good."

Louis yelled over the rising wind. "We need to get working on a shelter before the rain hits." He threw his bag over his shoulder and grabbed his fishing pole in one hand and black skillet in the other and walked toward the back of the clearing where there was a large rock formation. "Find branches—big, long branches," Louis said. "Go into the bush and bring them here. And hurry, that rain is coming in fast."

They all went hurrying into the trees and brush nearby, searching first for the easy pickings, those branches that had already fallen off the trees. With the larger pieces, they would get the base of the structure started. He suggested everyone cut fresh pine branches with the two hatchets they had brought along. The guides began to build and weave the shelter against a rock ledge. They also pulled up moss to cover and patch the roof in order to keep the rain out, especially where the branches met the rock. A tarp was thrown over the entire structure, and they crawled inside just as the first large drops of rain hit.

The sky overhead had grown dark, so it was also quite dark inside the shelter. Twelve bodies awkwardly huddled together in the tight space. Even though it was uncomfortable, it did prove beneficial for shared body heat. Grace was thankful for the warmth, and her shivering slowed over time as she sat, hugging her knees. Feeling tired and cramped between Nicki and Kat, Grace found the T-shirt she'd stuffed in her backpack before her impromptu swim, draped it over her legs, grabbed her backpack to use as a pillow of sorts, and lay down, curling up on her side. Closing her eyes, she listened to the loud crack of thunder that became a giant boom and eventually turned into a long, lingering rumble in the distance. With the tarp overhead, the flash of lightning was muted, but the intensity of the thunder assured them it was nearby. They listened to the storm overhead, thankful the largest of trees was elsewhere on the island and for the rock ledge that created a strong wall for their shelter and excellent protection from the elements.

Eventually, the storm quieted and conversation began with the beating of rain on their makeshift home. As Sebastian and Marc filled the group in on what they had found on the island, Grace sensed there was more to the story than what they let on. Whatever Sebastian said, Marc seemed okay with that version of the truth. Grace listened to stories of Alexander—or Xander—Fortin and his super-human abilities as she drifted in and out of consciousness. They certainly thought highly of their friend. She tried to stay awake but finally let the exhaustion overtake her, safe in the knowledge that she had people nearby who would wake her should there be any trouble. The last thing Grace remembered in her state of half-sleep was her name and some soft chuckles as someone said, "It's no wonder she's so tuckered out."

CHAPTER 9

Learn What It Had to Teach

—Henry David Thoreau

G RACE DREAMED OF WATER, LOONS, AND LOST BOYS. Figuratively and literally. Her subconscious knew there was more to Sebastian's story than met the eye, though she had no idea what that could be. Pushing back the heartbreak of the past months, Grace recalled a time when things were still good, normal. Of home. Then, of moving to Peterborough and rowing in the cold October air. There was frost on the dock, and Grace was so sick of the training and pressure that came with a long summer of competing.

Finally sinking into a deeper sleep, Grace saw herself in the arms of a man that held her and kept her warm. He told her it was going to be okay and that she didn't need to worry anymore. He would take care of her. Grace wanted to let him but knew she couldn't.

She heard a gunshot, and his arms fell away. She opened her eyes, and he lay on the ground where he had fallen, his face wide-eyed and blank. Grace screamed, but there was no sound. *He* grabbed her, and as she tried to shake him off, she woke with a start.

"Shhh . . . it's okay," a voice said to her. "You were dreaming."

Surfacing from the deepness of her dream, Grace opened her eyes and saw Cam looking back at her. She realized that Cam was the man who had just died in her dream. Shaken, she realized the truth of it. If *he* found her, anyone she cared about could be hurt.

As Grace tried to get her bearings, she asked, "What time is it?"

"It must be past midnight already. You fell asleep early," Cam whispered, lying on his side where he'd been sleeping only inches away from her. "Are you okay?"

"Yeah. Yeah, that swim wore me out." Grace tried to avoid any questions about her nightmare. Not wanting to wake anyone and not sure she should ask, she whispered, "Hey . . . question."

"Shoot," he replied without hesitation.

"Well, you seemed pretty upset when I got back to the island yesterday. What was wrong?" Grace picked at her cuticles, waiting for the reply.

His face clouded, and he opened his mouth to respond, then shut it.

"You seemed mad." She winced, wishing she didn't care.

"Well, I guess I kind of was." Her face stricken, he grabbed hold of her hand. "Wait, let me explain." She pulled her hand away but waited to see what he had to say. "When I got back to the clearing, people started trickling in. I was watching for you, wondering where you were. I didn't say anything at first," he said with a shrug. "Then Louis started talking about heading back. I pointed out that you hadn't returned yet, so he rang the cowbell and we waited a few minutes. He rang it again, and I started to worry."

"I'm surprised I didn't hear it." She shook her head. "I figured I was almost within yelling distance from the other island."

"Maybe the wind was blowing the other way."

Grace nodded, not wanting to break his train of thought. She looked at the vulnerability of his tanned neck and thought how nice it would be to kiss it, snuggle in, and breathe in his masculine scent. Grace saw stubble on his strong jawline and wanted to reach out to touch it. She jumped a little when her eyes wandered to his and found herself looking directly into his gaze.

He cleared his throat. "Anyway, I started jogging down the path I'd seen you take and looked into the water in spots where it opened up. I was worried maybe you'd fallen in or something. It wasn't long before I heard Jake calling me back saying they'd found you, so I ran back. Then I saw you coming across the water with those guys, and they made me uneasy." He shrugged. "I didn't trust them as far as I could throw them. I'm just glad they brought you back."

"W-Well, that's a relief." She chewed on her cheek before getting enough courage to say, "I thought you were mad at what I was wearing."

"Mad? No, of course not." He frowned. "Why would I be?"

She blushed. "Sorry, a weird thing to worry about. Unfortunately, that thinking has been ingrained on me over the last few years."

"What a moron," Cam summed up.

A companionable silence followed while Grace rolled onto her stomach to look around. Kat and Jake had curled up at the far end of the shelter with Nicki beside them. Kat must have crawled over top of everyone to get a little closer to Jake.

"Looks like Kat deserted me. Can't say I blame her. Jake'll keep her warmer." A shiver went down her back just then as she realized she'd been lying in a bathing suit and shorts on hard Canadian Shield for about four hours with only her sweatshirt for warmth.

Cam noticed. "I looked for a blanket for you, but Evelyn had already claimed the last one without realizing it. Marc and Sebastian had sleeping bags that they opened up at the far end for a few bodies to sleep on. I'm pretty sure they would have made room for you had you been awake, but to their disappointment, you were fast asleep and no amount of mentioning your name was going to change that." He chuckled.

Looking at the ceiling and shaking her head, she didn't say anything. Being the only single girl in a group of men made her stand out. *He* would've had a heart attack if he knew where she was. Still, feeling the pull through the dark, Grace wished Cam had a blanket to share with her.

"So, who got the other blankets?"

"Nicki has one. She had planned to share with you and had the blanket on you at one point, but it looks like she's a bit of a blanket hog." He smiled, eyes twinkling.

Her breath caught. He was just too cute. Grace glanced over at Nicki, and she was wrapped up like a caterpillar in a cocoon.

"There were three, and I think Kat and Jake snagged the third."

She squinted through the dark to see if he was right.

"Cody and Louis were fine. I guess they always dress in layers just in case, and I wore my jeans and brought along a sweatshirt, so I've been okay too."

Grace's muscles were taut from the cold, and her teeth had begun to chatter.

"Look," Cam said, "part of my duty as a member of this group is to keep fellow members warm when they're stuck on an island for a night, without fire, when everyone else has stolen the blankets. I swear I'll behave. You'd be doing Cody and Louis a favor, because it doesn't look good in the brochure when one of their customers dies from exposure."

"Okay . . ." She started blushing again, thinking about the possibilities. "What did you have in mind?"

"How about I put my sweatshirt on your legs?" He pulled it over his head, then yanked his T-shirt back down over his chiseled stomach that she had to pretend not to notice to keep herself from drooling. "And we sleep back-to-back. You can pretend I'm your dad or something. God knows I'll have to think of my toothless Aunt Edith to get through this myself," he said with a lopsided grin.

With his sweatshirt on Grace's legs and the warmth of his back on hers, she instantly felt better. Thankful for the body heat, Grace finally succumbed to slumber.

The repetitive caw of a crow overhead slowly brought her to consciousness. Grace must have turned in her sleep, because before she opened her eyes, she felt someone holding her. Her forehead rested against Cam's chest, and she felt it rise and fall in quiet breaths. She dozed again, and when she awoke, she was on her own with his sweatshirt tucked tightly around her legs.

The scurrying feet of a squirrel on their roof forced her to consciousness. Groaning, she rolled over and squeezed her eyes shut. Unable to ignore it, she propped herself up on an elbow and looked around. People were still sleeping. Extricating her legs from Cam's sweatshirt, she saw, thankfully, that he was gone. He'd seemed so mad yesterday when she'd gotten back from the island, and although he explained that he'd been worried, she didn't like it. She'd had enough of being judged, of being controlled, and didn't want to be anywhere near it again. Ever.

Needing to go to the bathroom, she tiptoed out of the shelter, trying not to disturb anyone. Cody opened his eyes as she passed, said a groggy good morning, and started to sit up.

"Go back to sleep," Grace whispered, motioning him to lie back down.

He gave her a wave of thanks and rolled over.

The morning was beautiful and calm. A water dance of loons sang their tremolo as they swam by the makeshift camp. Cam was bent over the fire feeding it a small twig. He gave Grace an easy grin; her heart hammered as she walked toward him. Avoiding his eyes, she said, "Here's your sweatshirt, thanks."

"Hope it helped," he said briefly, picking up on her mood.

She didn't have it in her to make chitchat just yet, so she nodded and turned without answering, making her way to a small path that led to the back side of the island.

Not wanting anything to ruin the beauty of the morning, Grace pushed all negative thoughts and feelings aside in an attempt to drive away the sickness she felt in her stomach. She had come for "me" time and needed to avoid anything overly emotional. Part of her was still in a state of shock. She'd gotten away and was terrified of the consequences.

Sitting down, she stared out at the water. Grace had loved getting on the water each morning at the boathouse and missed it. Letting her mind settle on the waves gently lapping the shore, she gave in to the peace and calm of the early morning.

In the distance, she heard a loud "Watch out!" as the makeshift shelter began to move and shake as if coming alive. The midsection collapsed to peals of laughter and cries of confusion. No major injuries and no harm done, their day began.

"Well, group, I think it'll have to be trail mix and tea this morning. The salami got finished off last night." Cody grabbed his backpack and secured it to his body. "But I promise you when we get back to the lodge, you will have the best breakfast of your life!"

"At least it'll taste that way to you starving folks," Louis humbly offered.

They sipped the tea while Louis doused the fire with water. Taking a stick, he gave it a stir, then walked back to get more water with the water-resistant bag he had kept the food in. Satisfied the fire was out, he shook the bag and began repacking it.

"You slept like the dead last night, Grace," Marc commented, trying to make conversation.

"Yeah, and your snoring could *wake* the dead," Sebastian added.

Nice. That's what a girl likes to hear. Real smooth.

"Where are you boys off to this morning?" Jim asked them, trying to steer the conversation away from their teasing.

"Well, now that we've got the coordinates for the next cache, I guess we'll head off and see if we can find box number three." Sebastian held the tracking device out in front of him as he tried to get a signal. "We may have to use our map to find it. I can't get my GPS working today."

"Hey, I forgot to ask," Nicki began, "don't people usually leave something in the cache for the next person to take?" Marc nodded. "Did he leave anything?"

"Yep, and yes, he did. He left something that would have made last night a lot more bearable." Sebastian smirked.

"What, a pillow?" Evelyn laughed.

"I wish!" Marc chuckled, stretching the back of his neck, chin to chest.

"Nah, a couple of ecstasy pills, but I wasn't sure this bunch would be okay with that." Sebastian cleared his throat.

No. Not comfortable with that, Grace thought.

She felt eyes on her as others watched her reaction. *Come on! There are others in the group, why look at me?* She refused to acknowledge it or make eye contact with anyone. *Back the fuck off, people.* Her mood darkened.

Joining the conversation, Cam said, "Does this look like an ecstasy-popping group?"

"Speak for yourself," Kat rebuked with a wink and some swagger, throwing the rest of her tea into the dampened fire.

"Hey now, it's a little early in the day for that, don't you think?" Louis cautioned.

"I'd say." Evelyn clucked, making Grace wonder if they thought it was okay in the evening. She smiled to herself and helped tidy up in preparation for their return to Thompson Lake.

Back at the cabin, Grace fell into her bunk and slept soundly until the breakfast bell rang. She ran her fingers through her tangled hair and decided to take a fast shower before going for breakfast. Afterward, she filled her plate and set a personal record for eating more eggs, bacon, and toast (washed down by strong coffee) than she ever had before, and began to feel human again.

"Well, we were planning on heading to the natural waterslides today, but after last night's adventures, I think we'll stick closer to home." Cody stood at the head of the table and looked around for signs of approval. "Feel free to explore the area around camp. Hopefully, you'll be inspired by the events of the last twelve hours or so."

"We'll meet back for dinner at six," Louis concluded.

Changing from flip-flops to sneakers in her cabin, Grace grabbed her journal and pen. "Nicki, what's your plan for the day?" Although she already knew the answer, as Nicki was in the corner frantically gathering up all her painting supplies.

"Well, I'm going to try to get some painting done. That island yesterday was just beautiful. I got some great shots while it was still sunny and some amazing ones of the storm. Yet, this lake here is just so gorgeous, I want to paint it too!"

"The pictures will be there when you get home. You'll just have to hold on to the feeling too," Grace suggested.

"Yes. Hey, I'm not going far. Would you mind bringing that little Bluetooth speaker on my bed there? I find I work better with a little background music."

Opening the door for Nicki and following her out, they walked a few yards past the firepit and down to a level spot sheltered by the trees overlooking Thompson Lake. As Nicki set down all her equipment and supplies, obviously distracted by what she wanted to accomplish that day, Grace said, "I'll see you later. Good luck."

"See you!" Nicki called back while unloading her canvas bag.

Smiling at her enthusiasm, Grace walked down the beach picking up pieces of driftwood and empty snail shells, the muskiness of the shallow water filling her nose. Moving up the bank and away from the shoreline, she found a flat rock in the sand. Inspired, she attempted to skip the rock and laughed when it hit the water with a plop and immediately sank. The disturbance caused the water to undulate out from the center, creating a ripple effect.

"That takes years of practice, you know," a voice said from behind her. Grace turned to see Cody walking toward her in his newly pressed button-up shirt. "Years."

"Well, no wonder it didn't work. I certainly don't have years of practice." She chuckled and observed him. He looked like he'd just stepped out of an Eddie Bauer catalogue. Olive green khakis, red plaid shirt, and brown Merrell hiking boots.

Sitting down in the warm sand and leaning back on her hands, she watched while Cody searched the sand for flat rocks. *He wasn't so bad,* she decided. *He just needs to stop trying so hard all the time.* Cody picked up a couple before lunging for another. "Oh, here's the one we need!" He walked over and showed Grace a bigger rock, about two inches in diameter, round but thin. "You've got to keep it flat so it doesn't grab the water when it hits."

"Du-uh," she said with a smile. "I know that. I just can't make it *do* that."

"Oh, sure you can. Watch." Cody threw the rock and made it skip four times. "Easy."

"Yes, super easy," Grace replied, eyebrow raised.

"Come on, give it a try." He grabbed her hand to pull her up, his deep brown eyes sparkling.

Grace popped to her feet, laughing. "Fine, I'll try . . ."

They searched for rocks along the water's edge, and Grace spent some time getting instructions on proper technique.

"Don't you have anything better to do than skipping rocks all day?" Jake shouted as he and Kat strolled hand in hand toward them down the beach.

"Hey, city boy, this is how I make my spending money." A mischievous grin spread across his face. "I'll bet you five bucks you can't skip the rock three times."

"You're on." Jake leaned down and grabbed a rock. Studying it in his palm, he flipped it over in his hand, stepped forward with his left foot, and tossed the rock with a snap of his right arm. The rock skipped one, two, and three . . . six times.

Cody laughed. "Double or nothing you can't do that again!"

"Deal!" Jake searched for another rock.

"And . . . that's our cue to exit," Kat said, rolling her eyes. Hooking her arm through Grace's, she led them farther down the beach.

"Where're you from?" Kat asked.

"Ottawa," Grace replied. "You?"

"Me too. Born and raised."

They walked in comfortable silence.

"Whereabouts do you live?" Kat asked.

"Well, my dad's in Orleans. I've been in Peterborough the last few years. Just moving back."

"Hey, if you need a place to stay, Jake and I are looking for a roommate," Kat offered.

"Really? Hm. I'll keep that in mind." Grace tried to sound interested and bent down to pick up a nice, flat skipping stone. "I'm going to have to figure things out when this trip is over." She examined the cool stone in her hand.

"How are you enjoying yourself up here?"

"Oh, it's beautiful. Not sure I fit in with the whole artists' retreat theme, but it's nice."

Noticing a pattern in the rock—black with white cracks in it that resembled a tree—Grace commented, "Hey, look at this. How pretty!"

Kat leaned in to see. "Cool! There is a tree and . . . this here looks like a river flowing into a lake. That'd make a great tattoo!"

"Maybe I should get one at the end of the week." Grace laughed. She had never considered getting a tattoo before.

"You should!" Kat clapped her hands and gave a little hop. "A reminder of your amazing week here and the start of your new life in Ottawa."

Grace chuckled, then looked at the ground as she digested that comment. Kat seemed to understand that this was a turning point in Grace's life.

"You and Jake seem pretty tight," Grace said, diverting the subject.

"We are. Soul mates," Kat confirmed.

"How did you know?"

"We just knew."

They walked a bit.

"You both look so comfortable together."

"We are. But you don't need to be soul mates to be comfortable with each other," Kat replied, her tattooed arm swinging as she walked.

"Tell me about your tattoos," Grace prompted.

"Well, this one was my first." She pointed to the butterfly on her ankle, then rolled her eyes. "Typical, I know."

Grace smirked.

"Then, I thought I would be a little more daring and started researching for this sleeve." She held out and turned her right arm so Grace could see it at all angles. "I love nature but didn't want too much color. Less is more sometimes—it leaves something to the imagination."

"I love it," Grace replied, examining the detail. There were geometric patterns, flowers, birds, and other references to nature—northern trees, the sky, and water—extending from her wrist all the way up to her shoulder.

"But my favorite is this." She pulled off her tank top and turned her back to Grace. "A lotus."

Amused by her lack of inhibitions, Grace looked at the artwork on Kat's upper back. It was a lifelike, three-dimensional flower in a pretty pink that sat just above her bra strap, between her shoulder blades. "It's beautiful," Grace murmured, wanting to touch it. "So realistic. What does it represent?"

"A lotus is a flower that can grow in dirty waters. They're a symbol of self-regeneration and rebirth."

Nodding, Grace walked down the beach as Kat put her tank top back on.

"Jake loves his tattoos too," Kat said. "He has a Welsh dragon on his left shoulder, some Celtic symbols here and there, mostly on his fingers, and a phoenix on his right shoulder and arm. The phoenix is a symbol of rebirth too."

Grace smiled, urging her to continue as they walked along the water.

"My dad hates my tattoos." Kat made a face. "He's pretty mainstream. Works for the federal government." She bent to pick a shiny white rock out of the sand. "He calls Mom and me gypsies. We are both a little too carefree for his comfort and we love giving him a hard time about it. He loves me, though." She offered a casual shrug. "I'm fun."

Grace laughed. "Yes, you are." She playfully bumped her shoulder to Kat's as they walked. "What about Jake?" Grace asked. "What's his story?"

"Oh, my sweet had it rough," she began. "His dad was an alcoholic, and his mom had trouble with it as well. He won't touch the stuff. Did you notice?"

No, I didn't, Grace thought as she shook her head.

"The guitar makes it easier for him. He doesn't want to explain that he's not drinking, so he accepts a drink and then doesn't touch it. People don't even question it since they figure he's just too busy playing to have it."

Kat took a few steps and picked some little purple flowers where the sand met the forest. Then a white one a little farther up.

"What do you do, Kat?" Grace asked, watching her.

"Oh, I am a jack of all trades. My real job," she said, using air quotes and trying not to drop her little bundle of flowers, "is working at a coffee shop near the university. I clean a few houses a week and paint house interiors—bedrooms, bathrooms, living areas, that sort of thing—when Jake needs some help with one of his jobs."

"Sounds nice. Not too intense."

"No, not intense, but exhausting and unrewarding at times. That's when I work on my poetry and Jake works on his music. It's always good to have a hobby that you love."

"Have you considered making it more than a hobby?"

"I have," Kat said quietly. "Maybe someday."

They continued to walk down the beach, enjoying the sound of the birds singing and the warm sun on their backs.

"You need to get that tattoo," Kat said suddenly, pointing at Grace's pocket where she'd put the flat skipping rock.

"Me? No, I was just kidding. It doesn't suit me," Grace replied.

"Says who?" Kat countered.

"Okay. Say I want one. Where would I put it?"

Kat looked sideways at her, thoughtfully, considering. "I'm not sure. I'll have to think on it. But you need one. One that maybe is just for you to know about. One that represents this time in your life. So you don't forget what you've learned."

Grace nodded, contemplating whether Kat could sway her.

Reaching the end of the beach, they turned and started to make their way back along the shore. They watched Jake and Cody in the distance. They were an unlikely pair. Cody was nodding enthusiastically, motioning with his arms, posturing and trying to impress, working hard to connect with Jake.

That was Cody, Grace was learning: he tried to adapt himself to whomever he was talking to. Well-intentioned but awkward, he came across as trying too hard. He lacked confidence, and Grace found herself wondering why. Kat ran ahead to try her hand at skipping a stone, and while Jake stood behind Kat, holding her wrist and moving her arm to give her a sense of the snap, Grace sat in the sand to watch.

Cody stood back watching and laughing along with them. Even laughing, he seemed unsettled, a fish out of water. He knew what he was doing at the camp—he was practiced at it—but maybe he wanted more. Noticing Grace, he walked over.

"What's up?" He tilted his head, aware that Grace had been watching him.

"I was just wondering about you." She gave a quick shrug. "How long have you been running the camp?"

Cody crossed his arms. "It's been six years now." Studying the sand, he said, "I started it after I finished school. Got a degree in marketing at Carleton with the plan of coming back here to run the camp." He glanced back at Grace.

"Are you enjoying yourself?"

"Yes, for sure," he answered, looking out over the lake.

"But . . . ?" Grace raised an eyebrow.

"But . . . I feel like I should be back there, in the city. And when I am there, I feel like I should be here," Cody admitted, his lips pressed together in a slight grimace.

"What do you love about the city?"

"Well, my little boy, for one," he answered, chuckling at Grace's surprised expression. "Owen," he offered, letting the information sink in.

"He's in Ottawa?" Grace asked.

Cody gave a nod. "Yes, with his mother."

Her back was getting sore, so Grace rolled to her knees and stood up. "Do you get along?" She brushed the sand from her hands and the back of her shorts.

"Well enough." Cody shrugged. "She understands me—she just wishes things were different."

"What does she wish was different?"

"That I would be better with commitment." He stuffed his hands in his pockets. "That I didn't love it here so much." He looked at the trees that met the beach.

"Why don't they live here with you?" Grace turned toward the lodge, arms crossed in front of her. They began strolling back down the beach.

"She's a city girl and she's moved on. She has a boyfriend and a job. Owen's in school now."

Grace looked sideways at his profile. "Couldn't they come and visit?"

He shook his head. "Nah, her man doesn't think much of me."

Nodding, Grace stayed quiet.

He picked up a stone and threw it. "Can't say I blame him." He gave Grace a small smile and headed back to the lodge on his own.

Seeing Nicki engrossed in her work, Grace took a detour to see how it was going. She tried to make out the song that was playing. "What are you listening to?" she asked, pointing at the speaker as she approached Nicki from the beach.

Nicki turned down the volume, holding her paintbrush in the other hand, then answered, "Styx, Boston, the Eagles. Older stuff."

"The Who?"

Nicki laughed. "Yep, they're on here."

"How's the painting coming along?" Grace stepped behind Nicki to take a look. She had painted a handful of pine trees leaning toward the water where the land jutted out from the natural line of the shore. Grace looked across Thompson Lake toward where Nicki was focusing her attention and saw the grouping in the distance.

"Good. I painted the undercoat of about ten canvases at home so they were ready to go."

"Always yellow?"

"Mostly if I want to represent a sunny, daytime painting. I've dabbled with red, pink, deep purple, but I like the golden yellow best."

"How many colors do you work with typically?"

"Hm, good question. It varies. Some paintings are simpler, straightforward, others I keep mixing and adding until it feels right."

"You have a great sense of color. Your painting is so vibrant. It's as though you take what you are painting and add 'happy' to it."

Laughing, Nicki replied, "No one has described it that way before, but yes, the colors I use do make me happy. If they don't, what's the point?"

She added a few strokes of a bright apple green to the foliage in the background.

"That's my absolute favorite color right there," Grace said.

"Yeah? It's a good one, for sure." Nicki kept her eyes on her work.

Letting her eyes linger on Nicki's painting in appreciation a little longer, Grace was inspired. Finding a spot nearby, Grace pulled her windbreaker over her head. Pushing back against a tree trunk, she pulled the lightweight jacket underneath her to keep the moisture from last night's rain from seeping into her clothing. She opened her journal and took the lid off her pen, flipped to a blank page, and again took in her surroundings to still her mind.

Breathing in through her nose and out through her mouth, Grace allowed her mind to clear. She felt the gentle breeze on her hair and the sun on her shoulders and watched the water twinkle in the distance. Ready, Grace scratched down words as they came to her.

The water beckoned as I walked along its sandy edge.
Stepping over roots and under branches,
it asked me how I was.
I stopped to look closer. "Why do you ask?"
I wondered. "Why do you care?"
Shaking my head, I continued,
holding my breath, listening,
to see if it would ask me more.
"She'll be fine," the tree spoke for her,
the water lapping at the shore in response.

Sitting still, she let that sink in.

Grace committed the view to memory. Hopefully the words would bring the moment back.

Stretching her neck right and left, she thought about Kat's "real job" and whether poetry would become a chore for her if she took it more seriously. Grace leaned back again and poised her pen to write.

Freedom.
Fleeting or forever?
We are always tied to the daily grind
one way or the other,
to make ends meet.
Our gifts become a chore.
Change the mindset.
Stay positive.
Look to the future.
Set your goals and meet them.
Choose freedom.

Okay, not quite as poetic, Grace thought. *It sounds more like advice from a life coach. Maybe that'll be my new profession.*

Grace glanced again at Nicki's painting. She had transformed it in the short time Grace had been there. The landscape was taking shape. She loved her style, which used bold, beautiful strokes. The perspective and depth came naturally to her.

> *Bold, beautiful colors*
> *Jumping off the brush*
> *Splashing, swirling, dancing,*
> *Forming a world of magic.*

Do poems have to rhyme? Grace decided that, no, they didn't. Smiling at her decision, she decided that was enough for now. Standing up and shaking off the twigs and soil from her jacket, Grace kept her journal open in case she was suddenly inspired again.

CHAPTER 10

In Dreams Awake

—Henry David Thoreau

G RACE SAT WITH HER EYES CLOSED, HER SUNGLASSES pushed to the top of her head to help remove the tan lines that had started to form around her eyes. The fresh air filled her lungs, and as Grace opened her eyes, she saw the peace she felt reflected on the faces of others in the boat. For the hundredth time that week, Grace thought, *I love nature*. She didn't think she could ever get enough of it.

Louis had suggested an impromptu outing to view a rock corridor not far off to the east. They jumped in the two fishing boats and made their way upriver. It was fascinating to see the unique passageway cut into the Canadian Shield. Grace watched the other boat troll beside and a little back of them while Cam and Louis tried to catch a few fish. They were in their element, talking and laughing as they cast and reeled their lines back in.

It was then that Grace noticed a lone man in a canoe coming toward their boats down the narrow corridor behind them. Cody put their boat in neutral while Louis moved to do the same on the other boat. Grace figured they were trying to ensure there was no wake. Later, she wondered if it was simply to allow the man to pass more quickly.

"This is one of the locals," Cody said in a low voice, his eyes on the approaching boat.

Margot already had her camera out and at the ready to take pictures of the cliffs, so she turned her camera toward the man in the canoe as he approached. She zoomed in, clicked, then paused and lowered her camera.

She glanced sideways at Louis, and he looked back at her with a sad smile.

Jim waved amiably and shouted "Good day!" to the approaching canoe. His wave slowed as he got a better look at the man and realized there would be no response.

Nicki gasped as he paddled alongside them. The waterway was narrow, maybe only fifty feet across at most, so his boat seemed very close, too close, as the madman floated by. His hair was matted, beard scraggly, and he wore torn thermal-base-layer leggings and a crew top and nothing else, not even shoes. He was strong and lean and looked like he lived in the woods on his own. Large as he was, his body was young and had not yet fully filled out.

His eyes were blank and glassy as he stared at the group. It was as though he was recording each of their faces to memory. She shivered and broke eye contact as soon as he looked her way.

"Hi, Simon," Louis said as they came level, and the man nodded to him before continuing on.

They waited until he was well beyond their boats and moving farther away. Then, one at a time, Louis and Cody put the boats in gear, made a wide U-turn, and headed for home.

Cody shouted above the motor, "That was Simon Mercer, a bit of a local legend and sometimes cruelly referred to by the locals as Sasquatch. He's harmless, really."

Strange to have such a normal name tied to someone so unsettling.

"That dude?" Jake asked. "Is he nuts or something?"

Cody adjusted his course with a slight turn of the wheel. "No. He and his parents used to come stay with us for a week or two every summer."

"But what is his issue?"

"Head trauma. He's slow to think, speak, and act. The bright light hurts his eyes." He squinted at the sun. "But he won't hurt you. Like I said, he and his parents used to stay with us every summer, and after one visit, he just decided to stay," Cody said.

"Being that this is a provincial park, how is it that he's able to stay?" Margot inquired, fascinated.

"He causes no problems and, in fact, has been known to help campers in trouble, with food or shelter. He even helped a family find their boat when it floated away on them one night," Cody explained, gearing the boat down. "He's not much for chitchat, but he is helpful."

As they beached the boats back at Dumais Lodge, already unnerved by their experience, the members of the artists' retreat found an unwelcome welcoming committee in Sebastian and Marc.

What were they doing here? Grace wondered, annoyed.

They reclined in the Adirondack chairs by the firepit. Their presence was upsetting, an intrusion to their refuge.

"Well, look who's here," Louis said stiffly. "How did you find us?"

"You'd said you were on White Spruce Road. Thought we'd stop by," Sebastian said with a smirk.

Grace found herself doing an inventory of what she'd left behind and made a mental note to go through her things to make sure nothing had been taken. Her life's savings was in her pack with her, thank goodness, so she knew that was safe at least. Grace didn't think they normally bothered to lock the main lodge, either. Given the lack of traffic in these parts, it would seem unnecessary.

The trip had taken a turn. It no longer felt like a glorious getaway for the group. With their night in the cold, wet wilderness, bumping into that wild man this afternoon, and now with Sebastian and Marc traipsing around the camp, they were left feeling uneasy.

"I see you've made yourself at home," Cody said, pointedly eyeing the drink in Marc's hand.

"Hey, sorry." Marc lifted the drink with a shrug. "I had to use the can, then I got thirsty. You have a great stockpile of booze in there."

"How'd you get into the cabinet?" Louis asked.

Marc shrugged. "Picked the lock."

Louis nodded slowly, hands on hips.

Sebastian leaned back in his chair, seemingly unruffled.

The two hosts looked at one another.

Cody's arms were crossed in front of him. With a shake of his head, he held his arms wide. "Okay then!" He took a cleansing breath. "Let's hope there's enough booze left to last us to the end of the week!" With a lighthearted laugh, Cody said, "Why don't you all grab yourselves a drink, and Marc and Sebastian can tell us about their day."

They made their way into the lodge and gathered in the kitchen. Cody flipped on the lights and opened a window to let some fresh air into the building.

"So, what happened with you two today?" Jim asked, addressing Sebastian and Marc. "What brought you here?"

"We found Xander's third box. Thought you all might want to hear about it," Sebastian answered.

Thought we might stop by for some free food and comfortable lodgings, Grace translated.

Louis went to the pantry for snacks, subtly checking that nothing else had been tampered with.

"You found the third geocache box, did you?" Jim's eyes lit up. "Let's have a look." He reached for the note in Sebastian's hand.

"Sure." Sebastian handed it to him with a scoff.

Margot snapped a picture as the note changed hands and another of the actual text over Jim's shoulder.

Jim read it and passed it to Kat, who read it aloud:

"3 — Rather than love, than money, than fame, give me truth."

—Henry David Thoreau.

Coordinates: 44.3822 N, 77.8361 W

"Xander was studying law," Sebastian offered, shrugging. "That fits with the truth part, but it doesn't really tell us much."

"Maybe he was just putting random stuff in there." Marc looked around for confirmation. "You have to put stuff in the box like you're supposed to."

"True, but could it be he was saying something else?" Grace mused.

"Absolutely. Look what he wrote on the back," Kat said.

Well, boys, there is a truth I want the world to know.
Can you guess what it is?

—Xander.

"Sounds kind of specific to me," Cam stated. "What kind of truth do you think he'd want people to know about?" He waited for Sebastian or Marc to respond.

Marc grimaced and shuffled his feet. "I have no idea."

Sebastian turned away from Cam and walked toward the living room. "How would I know?" He stared out the windows at the waters of Thompson Lake. "The drug he left this time was bizarre. Something we don't see here," Sebastian grumbled.

"What was it?" Grace asked, her interest piqued.

"It's called Devil's Breath," Marc said uneasily.

Sebastian turned back to them. "Otherwise known as scopolamine," Sebastian continued. "I wonder where he got it . . ."

Grace hated drugs. She hated what they did to people both on the streets and through the health-care system. She had seen pills, pills, and more pills while visiting her mom at the hospital.

"It's made from a plant that grows in Colombia and can come in the form of a fine white powder, like you've got there." Jim accepted the bag that Marc handed him. "Urban legend says you can be walking down the street, and if someone blows it in your face, you essentially turn into a zombie." He chuckled, handing the bag back to Marc. "I don't know if I believe that, but put it in a drink and it could cause the victim to lose their free will and memory of the events. It's been used for rape, abduction, theft," Jim explained. "I came across this particular drug early in my career."

"I think it has been used as a truth serum in the past," Cam added, leaning back on the kitchen counter, hands holding it on either side of him.

"Which kind of ties into the whole 'truth' part of the quote, right?" Marc offered, happy to contribute.

Staring at Marc, Grace gave a quick nod. "That makes sense. And that's what Xander left in the geocache box?" she asked uneasily.

"Yes," Sebastian confirmed. "But what does that matter?"

"Well, I was just thinking . . . Are these geocaches recorded on a website, or did Xander set up these particular caches himself?"

"He said he was going camping where he and his dad used to go every summer. We parked where they had always started and looked for the first geocache in that area through a geocache website. He was a cacher, and we hoped to confirm that he'd been that way. If he had signed the log-book, it would be the confirmation we needed." Sebastian clenched his jaw, wondering where she was going with her questioning.

"But the next one," Grace persisted. "Was that an offi-cially recorded cache, or was he setting the path himself?" She took a few steps along the length of the kitchen floor. "If he set them up himself and didn't officially record his caches, he could be pretty sure that no one would find the drugs or messages but you, or I guess, whoever found his first message." She looked to Sebastian. "Considering the messages are addressed to the two of you, I would bet that after the first message, he didn't use locations from the website. Why do you think he wanted you to find this?"

Sebastian shook his head. "I have no idea."

Grace stopped speaking. In the silence, Cam cleared his throat. "It does look as though he knew you would be looking for him from the start of the trip."

Jake pulled Kat closer to him. "I wonder why he'd go to the effort to have you come all the way here to look for him." He said what everyone was thinking. "And why this drug? It's not for recreational purposes like the others are."

There were murmurs of agreement and mutters of denial.

"So, if they were planned, what could this message mean beyond *give me truth* in a general sense?" Jim opened the question to the group.

After a pause, Jake suggested, "It sounds as though he had a 'truth' he wanted to reveal."

"Uh, Xander really likes love, money, and fame," Marc said.

"Well, then, if Jake is right," Margot said, "this truth must be pretty important to him."

The fire crackled and snapped as Grace stared into it that night. Exhausted and barely able to keep her eyes open, she still wasn't ready to head to bed. Some had packed it in for the day while others had gone skinny-dipping. She could hear the laughter and splashing in the distance. Swimming in the buff was not her thing, but unfortunately, it was their musician's thing, so there would be no campfire songs tonight.

Jim leaned back in his Adirondack chair, legs stretched out in front of him. "I started my training from the OPP back . . . let's see, just over forty years ago now." He pursed his lips as he spoke, staring at the fire. "And for a good chunk of that time, I've been interested in the history of Canada, particularly in the geographical areas where I had worked." He took a sip of his rye, served neat.

Nicki was wrapped in a blanket, and Margot sat across the fire listening. Evelyn sat to his right with Grace next to her.

"I started in smaller communities and worked my way up to the bigger centers." He looked at Evelyn. "I found it interesting to see how history repeated itself—so often." She nodded in agreement. "Humans are flawed, and no matter where I worked, I saw patterns."

"What kind of patterns?" Margot asked.

"Patterns of violence and abuse in poor economic times, not surprisingly. An increase in fraud as well. It got me thinking about what circumstances may have existed even prior to the establishment of Canada as a country." Jim moved his hands as he spoke. "That led me into the history of Canada in general."

Evelyn jumped in. "Jim would tell me about what he'd read, and sometimes it would overlap with what I knew from work. The history of a country isn't told through books alone. It can be told through art as well."

"Take the Group of Seven." She looked pointedly at Nicki, knowing she would understand. "They were a group of men who made a conscious decision to focus on the Canadian landscape, turning away from the European style of painting that was popular at the time.

"They focused on the northern boreal forest of the Canadian Shield and were also known as the Algonquin School because much of their paintings were done right here in Algonquin Park."

"That is so interesting," Grace said, pulling her foot up onto the seat of the chair and hugging her leg. She'd heard of the group and had always been curious about them.

"In fact"—Jim leaned forward—"there is some mystery and intrigue regarding one of the men, Tom Thomson."

"He painted one of my absolute favorites!" Nicki held her hands to her chest. "*The Jack Pine*." She put the back of her hand to her forehead, swooning in her seat.

Evelyn laughed. "I love that one too."

Grace turned to Jim from her seat, her eyes bright. "You said there's some mystery and intrigue surrounding him?"

"Yes. He was a skilled outdoorsman having spent much of his life in this part of the world." Jim swept his arm toward the lake. "Unfortunately, he died at the age of thirty-nine of an apparent drowning on Canoe Lake."

"Is that far from here?" Margot asked.

"I had to look that up." Jim shook his head quickly. "It's actually not. It's just south of here as the crow flies."

The conversation went to further talk of painting and artifacts. It was soothing just listening to everyone's voices. She stared at the flickering flames and didn't want the day to end. Last night, as uncomfortable as it was, Grace had found herself in a place surrounded by good people and potential friends. Unfortunately, in three short sleeps, they would all be heading in different directions again. But this time here . . . it seemed significant. Life-changing.

Grace thought about the geocache messages that had been found. They did not seem to be random messages. They were clues, intent on leading the searcher to the next box. She was curious as to what the final destination and treasure would be.

The fact that they were numbered could be important. The order in which they were placed might have some significance. She'd found number two on the little island. Sebastian and Marc had found the first earlier that day on their own via the geocache website. Marked with a "1," the coordinates on Xander's note had led them to Grace and essentially ended the possibility of anyone else following, given that they'd kept the note. The Thoreau quotes and personal messages from Xander were interesting. Were they meant to simply enlighten them to the world of poetry and allow them to look at life a little differently, or were the messages more calculated?

There was a reference to dying in the first note that unsettled her. She wondered if it meant anything, or if it was simply part of the text that couldn't be removed without affecting the entire passage. From what Grace could remember while dozing in their shelter on the island, Sebastian and Marc had said that Xander lived life to the fullest. If so, why would he be referencing dying?

There were more questions than answers.

What they did know was that he left home—Ottawa—one month ago and never returned. He'd told only one person, that they knew of, that he was going, namely Sebastian. He mustn't have mentioned it to his parents, or they would have reported him as a missing person and it would have been all over the news. In light of the messages being left intentionally right from the beginning of his trip, it would appear that Xander had something on his mind. But what?

Regardless of Xander's intent, it wasn't a good idea to travel in these parts on his own. He obviously hadn't watched *I Should Have Died*. There was a common theme on that television show. They all went into the wild *by themselves* to prove something. Not a good idea. People who go into the wilderness on their own often don't come back. *Look at Tom Thomson, for goodness sake!* People could easily get lost up here. Sometimes never found. Unless *he was* found . . .

Grace thought about their encounter with that strange Bush Man earlier that day, Simon. Just the thought of him gave her chills. He passed them all without so much as a hello. *What was going through his head?* Not a lot, she would bet. Louis said he'd had serious head trauma. *How might that affect his behavior?* she wondered. It was worrisome that he was out there, no matter what Louis or Cody said.

If a person was traveling on his own, like Xander, how would an encounter with this odd man go? Grace wondered. Would it be a non-event, like their interaction with him this afternoon, or would it be something more? She imagined Simon surprising Xander in the woods. Xander might have lashed out. If he'd angered Simon, the powerful man would be dangerous. He was remarkable, massive even, and would likely beat most anyone in a fist fight. She hadn't heard how big a guy Xander Fortin was, but the fact that his size hadn't come up in conversation told her he wasn't extraordinary in that way. And if Xander did manage to get away from a volatile situation, escaping Simon would be difficult. His tracking skills would likely be second to none given his time in the woods.

What is Simon Mercer really like? Grace mused. *And could he be responsible for Xander's disappearance?*

Regardless of what could happen to Xander, he had ensured he would be found because of the GPS coordinates left on the back of the notes. It would be nice if they led to a lovely, rustic cabin in the woods where he'd be hunting or fishing by day and playing solitaire by night, but Grace knew that wouldn't be the case. If he was okay, Xander wouldn't be waiting around for this game of hide-and-seek to come to an end. He'd be onto the next adventure just as soon as he'd laid the groundwork and then catch up with them at some point in the future to have a laugh. That could be one possible ending to this adventure. That would be a good ending.

Marc and Sebastian had said he was a law student who felt he could try any drug and not get hooked. He loved to share his experiences, describing the effects each type of drug would have on him. He was a showman, a natural athlete, charismatic, and exceptionally bright from the sounds of his entrance scholarship. He wasn't promoting the use of drugs—he was simply stating what his experiences had been. He approached them like a science experiment and seemed to think himself immune to their addictive properties, because he wasn't using them for relief or as an escape; rather, he used them to satisfy his inquisitive nature.

Is that all it took not to get addicted? One-time use only? She doubted it. But perhaps this ladies' man, this guy who had a bright future, could manage it. She hoped so for his sake. What a waste otherwise.

Grace looked around the fire and flushed when she realized the others had left without her noticing. Regardless, she was thankful for a distraction from her own worries and decided to indulge herself further. She tucked her legs under her and, resting her elbow on the flat of the armrest, put her chin in her hand.

Xander would have just finished his second semester, so the trip was likely just a break from school, a recovery from all the exams and a vacation before the next semester began. That made sense at least. She wondered how he had done on his exams. That would paint a picture of his mood going into the trip. Was it to celebrate or run from his problems? The answer to that question alone might allow for a decent prediction of the outcome of this mystery.

Gazing at the fire and scratching a mosquito bite on her ankle, Grace considered how Marc and Sebastian seemed to worship Xander. She didn't think much of Sebastian, and Marc seemed more of a follower. Xander might just be a big fish in a little pond.

"Headache?"

Grace jumped, not having heard anyone approach. It was Sebastian, the towel from his swim wrapped around his hips. She had forgotten that they were still there.

"No, just tired." She put her hand in her lap.

Ignoring her, he began massaging Grace's neck. "Here, this'll make you feel better."

Where is my crazy, jealous ex-boyfriend when I need him? "I'm okay, really," she insisted, turning in her seat to break the connection.

"Why don't you come into the lodge for a nightcap?" Sebastian said, looking down at her with a slow smile. "It's been a long day."

Grace knew a trap when she heard one. "Nah, I think I'll head to bed." Grace stood and began to walk away.

"Your loss. I make a mean hot toddy."

"I bet you do," she replied dryly, wondering if he'd ever spiked a drink before. She wouldn't put it past him.

CHAPTER 11

A Canvas to Our Imagination

—Henry David Thoreau

GRACE WOKE EARLY THE NEXT MORNING TO THE SMELL of pine filling the chilly morning air. Her subconscious had continued to puzzle through the mystery of Xander's disappearance during the night and had intertwined with memories of the last couple of years, leaving her feeling unsettled. She stepped out of the cabin and ran her hands through her disheveled hair before tugging her cap onto her head and setting her sunglasses on the brim in case the sun eventually broke through. Fog hung low over the lake, as the water had begun to hold the summer heat. It continued in patches over the beach and trailed into the trees. Grace buried her face in her hands as she walked, then let them slide down her cheeks to her chin before letting them drop to her sides. She carefully shut the bathroom door. Leaning forward to find the eyelash that was irritating her eye, she saw the strain in her pale face.

Aware that Louis and Cody were still asleep, Grace continued to hold her breath while she tiptoed back outside. Wishing she had a rowing scull to hop into, Grace instead turned away from the water in favor of the old logging trail.

She darted toward it, passing Marc and Sebastian's tent as the rain started to sprinkle down; she was trying to get away from her own nervousness, looking back as she went. It felt like someone was out there watching her. Grace walked faster and faster down the path, absently wondering how far this path would go, when she heard a snap and saw a blur to her left. Frozen to the spot, Grace peeked back again from where she'd come, wondering if she could outrun whatever it was and call for help before being caught. Ignoring the growl of her stomach and the pounding of her heart, she listened and tried to figure out what it was and whether she needed to worry. Was it a bear, a moose, simply a racoon or even a bird? Grace had been so lost in thought, she hadn't been watching more than the path in front of her. A chill went up her spine as she felt eyes on her—not imagined like maybe someone was watching. No, she knew someone was watching. Grace held her breath as her eyes darted back and forth, frantically trying to see through the dense vegetation in order to find confirmation that her sixth sense wasn't acting up.

And then she saw it. Two eyes peering back at her. They were unfocused, as though working on instinct. She had seen eyes like that recently. As her brain analyzed where it was that she had seen them, Grace realized they were looking down at her from a height of at least six inches above her.

She ran.

She pushed her legs to turn over; as soon as one toe hit the ground, she drove the other leg down until it got traction. Grace's arms pumped, and a memory from deep in the recesses of her mind surfaced. It was of playing capture the flag in grade school with her enemy tight on her heels, only inches away. Head down, Grace ran until her throat was raw, not looking back or knowing if she was being followed. Sunglasses and rowing cap had flown off her head the instant she had started running. Feeling the air whip by her ears, Grace had to blink the early morning rain out of her eyes.

The weather in the north tended to pass through more quickly than in the city. The clouds moved faster, and the rain fell harder, but it often passed on within minutes. As Grace ran, the rain pelted her and her feet began to slide. Beginning to tire, she slowed and decided to take the chance on looking back. If something were on her heels, it would give Grace the adrenaline she needed to keep going, or, if not, give her the chance to catch her breath. She saw nothing and felt nothing as she searched for firm footing.

Too close to the edge of the path, Grace tumbled down the side of the road some eight to nine feet, hitting brush and bouncing off trees, until her head hit solidly on the base of a tree and all went dark.

She woke to the sound of her name. It took a minute to focus, like it does when woken from a deep sleep. As she struggled to open her eyes, the brightness hurt them, along with her head, as she tried to sit up.

"Are you okay? What happened?" Cam asked, his forehead wrinkled as he looked back and forth between her eyes.

Grace's eyes widened, and she tried to sit up. "Something was chasing me! It was big! I saw its eyes in the trees looking down at me."

"What, an animal? A person?" Cam looked this way and that.

Putting her head into the palms of her hands, Grace let her hair fall forward to cover her face. "I must have been imagining things." She counted one, two, three beats as her heart raced in her chest. She shook her hair back out of her eyes and winced, then peered at Cam. "I am on edge. First, I couldn't get back on the island, then there was the storm, that weird guy in the canoe, and then this crazy treasure hunt Sebastian and Marc are on. Between all that and worrying about whether *he* will find me, it's all getting to me." Grace squeezed her eyes shut, her breathing quick and shallow. "How did *you* find me?"

Still kneeling beside her, Cam scratched Wolf behind the ears. Grace hadn't noticed him until then. "Wolf was whining and scratching at the lodge door. No one else was up yet, so I followed him. He must have known you needed help."

Wolf crawled up beside her and settled his head on her lap. As Grace rubbed his rough fur from the top of his head down his back, her breathing became steadier, but still she shook her head. "I don't know *what* I'm going to do next week." She looked at the muddy gravel road and felt the dampness seeping into her leggings. "Where am I going to go? What am I going to do?"

He squeezed her shoulder and stared straight into her eyes. "It's going to be okay. I promise."

Grace wished she could let him keep his promise, but she couldn't. It would be too dangerous for both of them.

Grace opened the door to the lodge, and Wolf pushed past her leg, the smell of bacon making him forget his manners. After explaining what had happened, a meaningful look passed between Louis and Cody. Louis examined her head. "That was likely Simon, the man we saw in the canoe yesterday. I'm sorry he scared you. He actually lives on our property." Speaking firmly, he said, "It's a bit of a debate that Cody and I have. *I* feel you should know, but *he* feels it makes people nervous. He has a point, so I haven't argued too much.

"Simon and his family came up here for a week every summer. Eventually, we'd let them take a canoe or fishing boat out on their own. He was a sweet kid, quiet. He played a lot of hockey in the winter, even to the end of June, so coming up here was a nice break from the rink.

"One summer when he was about . . . oh, I'd say fifteen, he came up and we could see right away he wasn't himself. He didn't joke like he normally did, and he spent a lot of afternoons in the cabin napping. I thought it might be the teenage thing, but his mom said that he had gotten a bad hit to the head at a tournament that March. In March, almost four months earlier!

"I guess it hadn't been his first, and he wasn't bouncing back as quickly. His grades had slipped—he just couldn't concentrate and he was frustrated. They hoped things would turn around for grade eleven." He stood. "Once he finally got the all-clear from the doctor, he was back at the rink and was able to get his driver's license and things started to improve." Louis looked at Cody to take over as the tea kettle began to whistle in the kitchen.

"One night after a late game just out of town," Cody explained, "his car hit some black ice and he rolled the vehicle. He was unconscious for two days, and when he woke up, he just wasn't the same.

"He managed to get through high school with some pity-passes and just passing grades. The teachers felt bad for him. They remembered the kid he used to be, confident, responsible. Instead, he had trouble getting assignments in on time, he would fall asleep at his desk, he rarely interacted with others, and his friends gave up trying to include him in activities, as he never went anyway.

"He fell into a severe depression after high school and couldn't hold down a job. They brought him up here the summer he turned nineteen, and it was the first time in a while they saw him happy. When it was time to head home, he wouldn't go. He took Wolf and walked down the logging road.

"We gave him some time, but after he'd been gone a few hours, I jumped on one of the quads and went looking for him. He'd gone to his fort that he'd built over the years. I figured that's where he would be. It's a couple of miles away, down the logging trail, almost directly across the lake from here. He'd been working on it all afternoon, clearing out old leaves, trying to make it a home, I think.

"Anyway, I convinced him to come back to the lodge for the night and promised I'd help him build a better fort." Cody held out a piece of bacon for Wolf to eat. "It was heartbreaking. He was so lost, and his parents didn't know what to do anymore.

"So, we all sat together that night and came up with a plan. Simon's parents would pay for and help build a small cabin that he could live in, at least for the summer months. We insulated it and put in a woodstove. There was no electricity there at first, so he came to the lodge to eat. Now we've put solar panels in, but he still doesn't have a well. He usually uses a filter and gets what water he needs from the lake. He pays his way by doing maintenance on the buildings and landscaping on the grounds around the lodge. It's a good arrangement." He rubbed Wolf's ears. "Wolf's become his dog as much as ours."

"We'd been talking about what to do today." Louis came back setting down a cup of tea in front of Evelyn. "I think we were leaning away from hiking the logging trail in favor of the waterslides. Either way, Grace, I don't think you should be going far today." There was a murmur of agreement and offers to stay back to keep her company.

"I'll stay back with Grace," Cam offered. "You all go ahead and have fun."

Ignoring Sebastian's smirk, Louis said, "That'd be great. We'll take both boats, and I will come back early to make my famous risotto dinner."

"Oh, Sebastian!" Grace had been meaning to ask. "Would you mind if I wrote down the messages Xander left in the geocaches? I'd like to read them over again. It'll give me something to do today." She held her breath.

"Sure, whatever." Sebastian pulled a face. "Sounds like a fun way to spend an afternoon." He snorted, reached into his back pocket, and slapped the crumpled papers on the table. "I don't need them anyway. I've got the coordinates for the next box already punched into the GPS."

"Okay, sounds like we have a plan," Cody said, and the group began to gather their things for the day.

Relieved that everyone had left, Grace watched out the window of the lodge as the red canoes paddled into the distance. While cloudy over Thompson Lake, it looked clear farther out.

"I'm going to head to my bunk," Grace called to Cam as she started to make her way through the kitchen to the door of the lodge.

"Ah, not a good idea," Cam countered. "You shouldn't be alone after that bump to the head, and you shouldn't sleep yet until we know how bad it is."

Grace stood, hand on hip, eyebrow raised. "Am I allowed to get my journal, or are you going to continue to tell me what I should do while I am not by myself, sleeping like I want to be?"

"Uh, sure?" Cam replied, wide-eyed.

Stepping out the back door, she shut the door firmly behind her. *I will not have another man tell me what to do!* Even if he was right . . .

Now where did I put it? Grace thought as she lifted her pillow and rummaged through her bag. *The locker!* She found her journal in the bathroom beside her overnight case, hidden by her towel. *I wouldn't have left it under the towel. It would have gotten wet. I could have sworn I'd put it on the left side of the locker. I really am losing it.* Shrugging, she slammed the locker door shut.

Back in the living room, she marched to the deep emerald green chair and pulled up the ottoman. Plunking herself down, she stretched one leg out and set it on the footrest, then crossed her ankles with the other before opening her journal, all the while ignoring Cam.

Not sure what had set her off, he kept his distance and settled into a chair on the other side of the room. He reached into the magazine rack and picked up a copy of the Algonquin Park newsletter, *The Raven*.

Grace flattened the pieces of paper from the cache that Sebastian had given her and reviewed the quotes again. She reached to turn on the floor lamp behind her so she could read it better in the cloud-darkened lodge.

"1 — I went to the woods because I wished to live deliberately, to front only the essential facts of life and see if I could not learn what it had to teach, and not, when I came to die, discover that I had not lived."

—*Henry David Thoreau*

Grace wrote in her journal.

What did Xander like about this particular passage? He, like Henry David Thoreau, went into the woods. In what way did he wish to live deliberately? Maybe it was just as simple as that: he deliberately went to the woods. Possibly for a specific, preplanned reason. He might have been saying that he went to the woods, canoe-camping, with the intent of considering his life, his purpose. He may have been hoping to make a decision of some sort.

Rereading the quote, Grace felt, from what she'd heard of him, that Xander didn't need to worry about not living enough in this life. He didn't let moss grow under his feet. But what puzzled Grace, worried her, was "when I came to die." Did he mean in the distant future or a more immediate one?

Glancing out the window, it looked like they might get some more rain. A cold rush of wind through the open window told her she was right.

"2 — If a man does not keep pace with his companions, perhaps it is because he hears a different drummer. Let him step to the music which he hears, however measured or far away."

—Henry David Thoreau

Grace thought for a moment. *Are there companions he can't keep pace with? Maybe his school friends? Or maybe he doesn't have any friends who can keep up with him. Given that*

Xander only let Sebastian know where he was going, maybe he's one of the companions he was referring to. But why him? Xander certainly marches to a different drummer than most. He does not sound typical, and perhaps that makes him feel alone. On this quest, he's marching to his own drumbeat, to his own music. Where is it taking him? That's the question that seemed to be consuming her.

Her hand cramped from all the writing. She gave it a shake.

"3 — Rather than love, than money, than fame, give me truth."

—Henry David Thoreau

She continued to write.

These messages are odd. A lot of thinking and planning have been put into them. But then again, maybe Xander just has a flair for drama. He may have had a book on Thoreau with him and on a whim used references from it to leave in the geocache.

Grace paused with the journal on her lap. Her head was beginning to spin. This treasure hunt he had set up fascinated her and had the added benefit of keeping her mind off her own worries. Off being hunted. Off feeling something for someone she should not be feeling at all.

Cam held his newsletter open in front of him as he read. Grace rubbed her forehead and closed her eyes.

Louis, true to his word, returned early, and she and Cam helped him in the kitchen.

"Didn't I read that you are a Red Seal chef?" Cam asked as he took glasses out of the cupboard.

"Oh, that seems like a lifetime ago . . ." Louis said with a wave of his hand.

"I've always enjoyed cooking." Cam walked the drinking glasses to the dining room table, passing Grace as she returned from setting out the plates. "My mom and I spent hours together baking cookies and making pancakes when I was little. In my teenage years, it was all about the pasta dishes. Cheap filler for a growing boy." He chuckled as Grace passed him again on his way back for more glasses, knives, and forks in her hands.

"Oh, look!" Grace strained to see out the window. "They're back."

While Louis finished cooking supper, they gathered in the lodge. They were tired after two hours of running up the path in order to go down the waterslide again. Margot showed Cam and Grace some photographs of what they had missed. The natural phenomenon looked amazing. The pictures showed water rushing down a huge rock formation, which had created a smooth slide after thousands of years of erosion. The slide appeared to be about twelve feet long and ran at about a 45-degree angle with a pool of water at both the top and bottom of the slide where you could stand or swim. The side of the slide rose up out of the water, creating what looked like a small hill that overlooked the waterslide, providing a warm spot to sunbathe.

Evelyn was unusually quiet. "Did you enjoy yourself today, Evelyn?" Grace asked.

"I did. Of course, I didn't join in the water sliding, but it was a unique experience just to sit and watch everyone slide down over and over again. It's quite the thing to have something like that naturally crafted." Her words were light, but her eyes were dull.

Jim seemed to sense Grace's question. "It was strange that Sebastian and Marc stayed as long as they did. You'd think they would want to continue their search for Xander."

"Exactly what I was thinking, honey," Evelyn agreed, her eyebrows squishing together.

"Well, I am pretty sure Marc was anxious to continue on," Nicki clarified. "He slid for a while and then told Sebastian they should get going, but Sebastian pretended not to hear him."

"Sebastian was a little off today, I thought," Margot said, offering up a rare opinion. "A little hopped up, on edge . . ."

"Or high," Cody grumbled.

Kat nodded. "Oh, for sure."

"Well, I'm glad they continued on their way, and I hope they don't show up here again." Cody moved his hands as though that was the end of their association with them. "I meal-plan for exactly the numbers that sign up, no more, no less. I don't like waste."

They enjoyed a wonderful dinner of chestnut soup, mushroom risotto with chicken breast, and asparagus, complemented by a chilled white wine from the Niagara

Peninsula, south of Toronto on Lake Ontario. After dishes and showers, the group gathered around the campfire again.

They were pensive as they watched the fire. Some had blankets wrapped around themselves as armor against the cool night.

"I think that full moon is messing with me again, Jim," Evelyn said, pulling the blanket tighter around her body.

The circle looked at her for an explanation.

Jim answered for her. "The moon pulls at liquids, whether it be the ocean tides or the water in our brains. Nurses in labor and delivery notice a jump in women going into labor. Remember that, Ev? When we had Emily? They laughed when we came in and said, 'Yep, definitely a full moon tonight.'"

"I often feel 'off' on the evening of a full moon," Evelyn explained, her shoulders slumped. "Anxious for no reason."

"I've heard the term 'lunatic' comes from the moon's effect on a personality." Cody leaned forward, warming his hands by the fire. "Some people are easily angered and have been dubbed lunatics, or 'luna-tics.' *Luna* is the Latin name for *moon*," Cody said a little sheepishly, hoping he wouldn't offend her.

Grace watched Cam as he stoked the fire.

"All I can say," Jim continued, "is that I don't sleep well during a full moon. Whether that's because I am affected by Evelyn's mood or it's affecting me in a somewhat different way, it's consistent."

"I read somewhere that a normal brain has eleven pounds of pressure on a normal day and twenty-two during a full moon. More pressure on the brain means more pressure on the hypothalamus, which controls our moods. Makes sense to me." Kat shrugged, then went back to massaging Jake's temples.

"I've heard animals are more aggressive during a full moon too. I suppose the effect on them would be similar to the effect on humans." Cam set the poker down and eased back into his seat.

A wolf howled in the distance.

What, were they everywhere? Grace had heard one on their first outing.

"That reminds me," Louis said with a half-smile, "make sure you don't leave any food outside tonight for anxious, sleep-deprived wolves or bears."

The group murmured a few yeses.

Making a mental note to go to the bathroom before bed, Grace leaned back in her chair, looking up at the moon.

"Oh, hey, who's up for Baileys s'mores?" Cody asked. "They're perfect for a night like this."

Louis stood up. "Good idea."

"What's in a Baileys s'more?" Nicki asked.

"It's Irish cream, crushed graham crackers, mini-marshmallows, and chocolate sauce," Cody explained.

"We'll bring one for everyone," Louis said.

"I'll come," Cam said. "Anyone need a refill?" He pointed his finger at each member of the retreat, counting the raised hands. Jake and Kat stood to lend a hand.

In the quiet of the night, the rest of the group stared at the fire.

Nicki kicked Grace's foot with hers. "How're you doing, honey?"

"Oh, I don't know. Hanging in there, I guess. I love it here. I don't want to leave," she replied, voice cracking.

"Boy, do I know what you mean," she continued pretending she didn't notice that Grace's voice had quavered. "The time is flying. I miss my boys, but time to myself is just so precious." She paused, savoring the moment. "What are you going to do at the end of the week?"

"I haven't a clue," Grace admitted, still staring at the fire.

"Well, don't be afraid to ask for help. You don't have to be alone in this."

"I'm not really good at asking for help."

Nicki patted her back. "How about just being open to it then?"

Grace nodded.

"I'll try. It's just that I don't know who to trust or what's right for me anymore."

"All I know is that you need to trust your instincts and guard your heart—protect it and only give it to someone who is worthy. It takes time to know whether someone is worthy or not."

Grace let the words sink in.

"Know what you want and don't bend on those things that are truly important to you. If you need a good communicator, don't take anything less. If you need hugs, make sure he is a hugger at heart, not just for show." Nicki pulled her feet up and held her knees to her chest.

"Is good important to you? It takes a confident man to be good. So many do what they think they should. A good man is grounded. He doesn't need to be the center of attention, either. That being said, an outgoing man isn't necessarily bad."

"Being quiet myself, I always felt I should be around someone who is outgoing to balance things."

"That's not necessarily the right fit. Sometimes it's more comfortable being with someone like yourself who understands your shyness and quietly supports you to come out of your shell when the time is right, and not before. Take it from me, I've made a few mistakes."

Grace smiled.

"Oh! Here's another mistake I've made that you should consider." Grace laughed as Nicki held up her pointer finger. "Not all people are wired the same way. Someone who appears normal and innocuous on the outside may be more complicated and different than you might expect once you get to know them. What I am saying is, don't jump in too soon. It's easier to get away once the alarm bells sound if you haven't gotten into things too quickly."

Grace threw her hands up in the air and laughed again. "Where were you a couple of years ago? I learned that one on my own." Her reaction caught Evelyn's eye, who turned to listen in.

"That's why we have boyfriends and breakups. You know, they say the pain of a breakup gets better in time, and that's true. For now, stay strong, take time for yourself, and really get to know yourself. It's important to get happy on your own. That's when good things start happening."

"Thanks." Grace couldn't help but beam as Cam came out of the lodge with his hands full of drinks. She wondered if he would be willing to give her the time she needed, then she smiled wistfully.

"I'll get off my soapbox now." Nicki chuckled as she accepted the decadent-looking beverage. Cam passed a Baileys s'more to Grace as well.

"None for me, thanks, Cam." Evelyn held up her hand with a quick shake of her head before turning to Grace. "Trust your gut, Grace," Evelyn said, lowering her voice as Cam made his way to deliver drinks to others sitting around the fire. "You know how bad things can get, and I'm pretty sure you won't let that happen again. Your eyes have been opened, and that knowledge will never go away. But remember, don't feel you have to follow a rulebook. All's fair in love and war, chickadee," she said with a half-hug as she stood to go. "G'night!" she called, giving everyone a wave. She leaned down to give Jim a kiss on the cheek and walked off to bed.

What am I going to do without these people at the end of this trip? Tears pricked Grace's eyes, and she squeezed them away. There would be plenty of time to cry later.

CHAPTER 12

Step to the Music

—Henry David Thoreau

G RACE HADN'T LET HERSELF THINK TOO MUCH ABOUT her past over the last day or two. There had been enough excitement to keep her mind busy. Now, she let herself wonder if *he* had been able to track her. Does he know that she went to Ottawa? Would he be flashing pictures of her to passersby on the street? Has he come upon the bed and breakfast?

If he had found the bed and breakfast, and if the woman there did identify Grace as being someone who had stayed there, would she mention the phone call she had made? Even if she didn't, he would observe the lobby and might even look at the pamphlets just as Grace had.

He might zone in on the very same pamphlet on Northern Adventure Tours that she had. Would he see the date of the excursion? Would he put two and two together? It was a long shot that he'd even find the bed and breakfast, but it could happen. Grace sat up in bed and looked out the window down the road back toward the way they'd arrived.

With that weighing on her mind, along with all that had happened this week—from the strange messages

Xander had left, to the frightening man in the canoe, and everything in-between—she had every right to feel anxious. Without the help of the full moon.

After showering, Grace went to grab some breakfast. There still weren't many up yet, but as she walked into the dining area, she noticed that Marc and Sebastian were back again. They sat eating at the far end of the table.

"How'd you sleep?" Cam asked as Grace sat down across from him.

"Actually, pretty well, all things considered. I guess I'm not affected by the full moon." Grace smiled wryly, taking a sip of coffee.

"And I didn't turn into a werewolf, so that's good." He smiled big, and her cheeks flamed crimson.

"Hey, there was no talk of werewolves last night."

"I know. I didn't mention it. There was enough creepy stuff already yesterday."

"Well, thanks. Now I'll have something new to think about tonight," she said.

"Good morning." Louis stopped by the table to add a fresh piece of French toast to Grace's plate. It was wonderfully warm and was sprinkled with icing sugar. Grace covered it with maple syrup tapped from the nearby trees last spring.

"Looks like Marc and Sebastian have become part of the artists' retreat," he said, leaning in and tightly nodding his head to the right.

Grace looked down to the end of the table where their plates were piled high with food. They were visiting with

Jim and Evelyn. Marc and Sebastian slouched over their breakfasts, giving brief answers to Jim's questions. Marc's face was sunburned a bright red, while Sebastian's arms were covered in dirt and scratches. There was a new rip in the side of his shorts.

"When did they get back?" she whispered.

"Late last night. They got lost and couldn't find the fourth box."

Taking a bite of French toast, she listened in.

"How long have you boys been in the bush now?" Jim asked Marc.

"We got up here on Sunday," he replied.

"Do you know what you're doing out there?" Cody asked from the other end of the table.

"Not really," Marc admitted. "We went out with Xander a couple of times in the past but only for long weekends. So, I guess three nights was our max. We just finished night . . . six. A new record." He gulped down some coffee.

"We packed lots of dried salami and cheese, chocolate and nuts. That diet gets old fast," Sebastian said, gobbling up more French toast in between words.

"Hmm. That would explain why you've eaten two days' worth of bread with all the French toast you've had," Louis grumbled as he sat down with his plate of food.

"Yeah, thanks, this is great." Marc stuffed in another bite.

"So, are you heading back out to look for that next box again?" Jim asked.

"Yeah," Sebastian said slowly, "we are, but this one's a little farther north. We tried to get to it yesterday but couldn't make it through."

"Which way did you go?" Louis asked, curious now.

"I'll get the map out and see if we can find you another route to try," Cody offered.

After bending over the map for a few minutes with Louis, Sebastian, and Marc, Cody straightened and reluctantly said, "Well, looks like you're headed our way today. Why don't you travel with us as far as Moose Bay and then continue on from there? We'll be there for at least a couple of hours before we head north to the Painted Cliffs. Your box is just north of there, so we may see you again before we head back to the lodge for the night."

Grace stood to take her plate back to the kitchen.

"Can't seem to shake those boys," Nicki whispered to Grace as they passed.

Sebastian and Marc really were bringing the positive vibe down. Grace poured herself another cup of coffee. Everyone was looking a little worse for wear this morning.

Sitting back down with her coffee, Grace took a sip as Jake and Kat made their way to the table. "How is the poetry and music going for you two?"

Jake snorted. The couple sat down with their coffees and plates. "I can't say that it's been going all that great," Kat replied. "I was hoping the rush of the natural waterslides would get the creative juices going. Instead, it just wore me out."

"Today will be better." Jake kissed her forehead, then reached for the butter and syrup.

"We've got a lot to do today," Cody said as he walked to the kitchen. "We'll paddle to the island at Moose Bay this morning and then go to the Painted Cliffs in the afternoon, so let's head out a little early if we can. How about we meet by the canoes just before nine?"

Grace brought along her journal and waited for people to congregate by the canoes. She was looking forward to writing some more poetry. She was also itching to get on the water again too. It was so peaceful and separated her from the possibility of *him* showing up.

Cody and Louis shuffled the boats up again. Nicki and Grace were put together this time. Margot and Cody, Louis and Cam, Jim and Evelyn, and Jake and Kat were the other pairings. Now that the group knew each other, it was nice for the couples to have some time together. Margot was using the time with Cody for additional research for her article. Grace wondered if she would ride back with Louis at the end of the day to get his perspective on things. Growing up in the north as he had would give Margot unique insights on the area.

Once they had found their rhythm on the water, Grace searched for a way to get people interacting again.

"You know, I kind of ruined two truths and a lie the other night," she confessed with a self-deprecating smile. "Did anyone want to continue with that? There are a few we haven't heard from."

"Hey, that's a great idea," Cody said. "Okay, we heard from Grace, Jake, Kat, Jim, and Margot. That leaves Evelyn, Nicki, and Cam."

"What about you and Louis?" Cam countered.

"Well, we're boring," Louis deadpanned, "but if you insist."

They tried to keep the canoes close enough so that everyone could hear, but it was difficult. They naturally broke into smaller groups, but the game continued and made the time to Moose Bay pass quickly.

They learned that Nicki's grandmother had also been a painter, heavily influenced by the Group of Seven. Evelyn shared that she had been married to Jim for thirty-nine years and together they lived in a two-story, not a bungalow, and doted on seven grandbabies to date. Cam confessed his love of music even though he's tone-deaf and has never picked up an instrument. He has a younger brother and works for CSIS, the Canadian Security Intelligence Service, as an intelligence officer. Cody, an only child. Louis, fifty-eight years old. The two of them had known each other Cody's whole life. As second cousins, they've kept one another sane at family functions by escaping the crowd and going fishing whenever they could. They never got in trouble for sneaking off, as the family would always be thrilled with their catch. Marc and Sebastian listened and contributed as well.

Evelyn's career had primarily been at the National Art Gallery of Canada. She held her paddle midair over the side of the red canoe and spoke with a bright, open face. "It's on the banks of the Ottawa River, right next to Parliament Hill and the market. A pretty idyllic place to work if you ask me." Grace had noticed a little quirk of Evelyn's. She couldn't talk and paddle at the same time. "I've been there longer than most, including the janitors, and have been lucky enough to work in most areas in many capacities." Evelyn's voice was light. "I started right out of high school and did whatever I was told to do from cleaning to photocopying. Eventually, I was trusted to work with the art itself as it arrived or left the facility." Evelyn set her paddle on her lap, and Jim switched to the other side of the canoe to keep their course. "I assisted curators in various departments and moved from drawing and sketches to sculptures and paintings as they needed me. I took training along the way and filled in the gaps once the kids were old enough. It's been a wonderful career. Walking in the front door of that building every day is so inspiring."

As they paddled along, Grace considered that world. It sounded heavenly.

Nicki gave a nervous laugh. "I don't think I'll be sharing my paintings with you here this week."

"Too late, I peeked!" Evelyn laughed.

Nicki groaned.

"There is absolutely nothing to be embarrassed about," Evelyn said. "You have real talent. I would love to see more of your work."

Glowing, Nicki said, "I began a blog of all my work to date, so I could show you those."

Eyebrows raised, Evelyn nodded. "Have you managed to sell some of your work?"

"Yes, I sell my paintings online, as well as through personal connections, commissions, and art galleries."

"Sounds like you have quite the career going already."

"I do struggle to keep up with demand at times, but I need to make hay while the sun shines, as they say."

"Who says that?" Grace laughed.

"Well, my grandmother, for one." She tilted her head back and looked skyward. "Probably no one else, but me nowadays." Nicki chuckled. "I just mean, I better keep working while the opportunity exists. If there are no paintings to buy, there are no paintings to sell."

"How long does it take you to finish a painting?"

"The little ones, two to three hours. The big ones, days. Weeks if it isn't working. Sometimes I just need to take a break and come back to it."

"Do you paint from home?" Grace asked.

"I do, but I prefer to work at the studio."

"A studio? Where? Outside of your home?" Kat called from her canoe, head turned and leaning as she strained to hear.

"Yes, it's on Waverly Street along the canal in a neat old home," Nicki shouted back. Glancing back at Grace, she continued, "There are about five or six other artists each renting a space."

"Sounds wonderful," Grace said, growing quiet.

They paddled in comfortable silence. There was a gurgle that radiated from the bottom of the canoe as the boat moved through the water in a rhythmic pattern of plops and splashes. The odd paddle would thunk against the gunwale in a misplaced stroke. The trickle of sweat that had run down Grace's back was cooled by the fresh air of the northern park.

"Jim, what do you do with your time now that you've retired?" Nicki asked.

"I write. I write about my time with the Ontario Provincial Police and sometimes tie it into pieces of Canadian history that I've researched," he replied. And with that, he and Louis began a discussion around the history of the OPP in the area.

Marc and Sebastian were quiet. When spoken to, they answered with brief statements. They sat stooped in their boat, their hair unwashed and messy. Sebastian had dark circles under his eyes. The search for Xander had worn them down, and while Marc wanted to keep looking, Sebastian had started to give up. Grace had a feeling that if they didn't find anything today, it would be time to pack it in and let the police know what they had found so far.

Upon arrival at Moose Bay, Cody gave Sebastian and Marc a wave. "Good luck finding that geocache box today!" As the members of the artists' retreat stepped out of the canoes and stretched their backs, they felt the tension recede as Marc and Sebastian faded into the distance.

With a flourish, Louis said, "Welcome to Moose Bay! All the amenities you require: a fire, seating, a bathroom . . ." He swept his arm toward the ground and the bushes. "Well, all that you require for the morning, anyway." He chuckled. "Make yourselves at home. We'll meet back here in an hour or so. Listen for the bell."

They separated, going this way and that. There were paths curving around the outside of the island and a few through the center. It was small enough that you definitely couldn't get lost. Grace figured she could probably walk around the perimeter in twenty minutes or so.

"Hey, wait up!" Grace turned to see Cam half jogging toward her.

She stopped, pleased but uneasy.

"Mind if I join you?" he asked.

"Sure. Are you going to work on the art of fishing?" she teased.

"Yes, I take my craft very seriously," he said, with a poker face.

They walked along the narrow path, Grace just a little ahead.

"Well, I'm becoming far more experienced with my pen and paper than the average person. I plan on making a living on these words of wisdom when I get back." And with that statement, Grace felt her stomach lurch. *Ugh. Back where?* she wondered.

As if reading her mind, Cam asked, "What *is* your plan when you get back?"

Grace looked at the ground as she continued to walk, her forehead wrinkled in thought. "I don't have a clue, actually. It wouldn't be smart to stay in Ottawa and hang out around where I grew up. Besides, no one is there anymore." She shrugged. "My friends have moved, and I can't go to my dad's. *He'd* find me there."

"Can't you go to the police?"

"He *is* the police."

"But . . . I'm sure they can help you in some way. Maybe get you into witness protection," Cam replied cautiously.

"Maybe, but what if he sees me in the system?"

"I don't think that's possible. Have you considered asking Jim? He might have some experience with this kind of thing."

Feeling a pang of relief, she said, "You're right. I need to talk to him about this. Though I hate to be a nuisance."

"You wouldn't be a nuisance. Didn't he already offer? I can talk to him for you if you want."

"No, I will do it." Grace groaned and leaned away from him.

"There's nothing to be embarrassed about," Cam said.

"Yes, but I let this happen to me. I got into this situation." Her chin dipped. "I am a terrible judge of character."

"Hey. None of this is your fault. You've got to remember that."

Grace forced a smile and nodded slowly.

"I'm not sure what the future looks like right now. I can't even get a job without him finding me." She sighed. "What a mess."

"One step at a time. Let's see what Jim has to say first."

They'd found their way to a spot where the path widened and delivered them to the water's edge. They faced each other as they finished talking.

"Okay," she muttered. "I'll talk to Jim."

"And, hey, if you need a friend, I can be that for you. You don't have to be alone in this."

Grace tore her eyes from his. She gestured to the water. "This looks like a good fishing spot for you."

"It does. Too bad you don't have a camera. You could put it to use and take some action shots of me." He posed for the imaginary camera as if he were a pro.

She chuckled despite herself, and it felt good.

"I left my phone at the bed and breakfast I stayed at the night before we left on this trip." Grace pressed her lips together and pulled them to the side.

Casting his line out with a twist of his body and a flick of the wrist, he replied, "I'm sure they'll set it aside for you."

The next half hour flew by as Grace watched Cam fish. It was great to hang out with someone who wasn't judging or criticizing her. For the first time in a long while, it felt good to be *her*. Cam made Grace feel as though she was interesting and special and strong. He didn't once put her down. Not once. He asked Grace about where she had grown up and what activities she'd done as a child, and she learned a little more about him too.

"So, you work for CSIS, do you?" Grace asked, as Cam cast his line into the water. She leaned back on her hands, legs stretched in front of her, her toes looked like they were touching the water.

"Yes, I started there right after college."

"What do you do there?" She knew nothing about it.

"Analysis mostly." He shrugged. "I watch for threats to Canada's national security and provide options on what might be done to avert them."

"That's impressive," she said.

He chuckled, casting his line out again. "Thanks."

After a while, things grew silent. Comfortably at first, until Grace began to think of that dance again. They had swayed to "The Dance" by Garth Brooks. How did the words go? Grace decided to google the lyrics. She reached for her phone in her pack, then remembered she didn't have it. Knowing she would never remember all the lyrics, she instead reminded herself of the tune. She thought back . . .

Warm feelings flooded back at the memory of dancing with Cam. Grace knew the lyrics hadn't fit their situation perfectly. Still, it had seemed beautifully romantic at the time, and since she was never one to really listen to the lyrics, it hadn't mattered. It was a song that somehow fit everyone's life, everyone's experiences.

Cam had looked puffed up and happy when they'd danced together so long ago. His eyes were brimming with excitement. That she could make someone so happy had made her feel special. Grace's stomach had done cartwheels at the time. She had been in awe that feeling that connected could happen so immediately with someone.

The pain the song mentions described the angst she felt walking away from Cam. And, yes, also the pain of wishing she'd done things differently was worth those few minutes with him. "The Dance" was their song.

"Lunch should be ready soon," Cam had said, but she hadn't heard. He turned to see why she hadn't answered. He saw her expression and set down his fishing rod. He walked over to her. "Grace?" He pulled her chin up to him. "What is it?"

"Oh, I was just thinking," Grace said, looking at him with warmth in her eyes.

He smiled back and, grabbing her hand so she could stand up, said, "Ready to head back?"

Nodding, she stood and started walking back the way they'd come. Cam followed, fishing rod in one hand, tackle box in the other. As they neared the gathering spot, the dinner bell sounded, startling Grace.

Stepping into the clearing, they saw that the group had already begun to fill their plates. Glad that they were distracted, Cam waved Jim over so they could speak privately.

"What's happening?" Jim asked, all business.

"I don't know what I'll do when this week is over," she began. "I need your help."

"Grace, do I have your permission to track him?" Jim jutted his head forward and looked her squarely in the eye. Grace didn't answer. "I need his name. If he's after you, I don't see how it could hurt for him to know you've asked for help."

"It's just that . . . He always said if I left, he'd kill me. If I threatened his career, he'd kill me slowly." Eyes unfocused, she said this as though repeating something she'd known for a long time and had thought about often. The men hadn't responded in any way, so she turned to see what they thought should be done. Jim stood, eyes toward the ground, as he struggled to process what he had heard. Cam was frozen to the spot, the vein on his neck pulsing. They were horrified, angry . . . furious. These good men cared, and suddenly Grace was glad they were on her side.

Jim shook his head. "There are so many bad cops on the force, this isn't unusual. When I see how and who they bully, it shocks me every time. But I'm not worried. We will stop him. I will need his name though, Grace."

Grace sat in silence for a moment weighing the options, the odds.

Jim added, "Grace, if you give us his name, I can get in touch with some very good friends of mine. Trustworthy ones. Men I've known for forty years and would trust with my life. They know how to deal with guys like this, and if we work together, he doesn't have a chance. We are trained for this kind of thing too."

"It's called 'How to Deal with Bad Cops 101,'" Cam said, straight-faced, trying to break the tension.

Grace let out a choked laugh before tears began streaming down her cheeks. She buried her face in her hands to hide the hysterics that were bubbling to the surface.

Jim put his hand on Grace's back to calm her. Cam held her hands in his and said, "Breathe, Grace, breathe."

They waited a few minutes for her to calm down, and when she did, Grace gave them what they needed to give her the best shot at surviving this.

"Jason. Jason Kovacks."

CHAPTER 13

I Fear No Danger

—Henry David Thoreau

JIM EXCUSED HIMSELF AND, PHONE TO EAR, DISAPPEARED down a path covered in thick, green foliage.

Cam watched him leave, then he turned to Grace. "Okay, that's all we can do for now. Let's get you something to eat."

"Everything okay?" Louis asked as he filled their empty plates with the freshly battered fish, fries, creamed corn, and warm maple beans.

"Not entirely, but it will be," Cam said. "Hey, how many outfitters are there between here and Peterborough?"

"Well, that depends," Cody answered, walking over to join the conversation. "Why?"

"I need you to contact them and get them to let us know if anyone asks about Dumais Lodge or Thompson Lake," Cam said.

Cody looked from Cam to Grace. "Is this about your ex-boyfriend?"

Grace nodded and let out a long, slow breath.

Louis paused before speaking. "And you think that he might figure out that you're up here with us?"

Everyone stopped to listen.

Cam rubbed the back of his neck. "Jim is on the phone right now getting some of his OPP buddies to try to figure out where Jason, Grace's ex, is at the moment. Hopefully, they'll be able to track him down and keep an eye on him." He crossed his arms and gave a quick tilt of the head. "But I was thinking that if we had a picture of him, we could send it to the outfitters and they could keep an eye out as well."

Jim had emerged from the path some thirty feet away and listened as he walked toward them. "And," Jim said with lowered brows, "they need to alert *us* should an individual matching that description show up asking questions—not 911, not the local police. It'll give us a heads-up that he's coming this way."

"What will we do if that happens?" Grace asked. "We can't let him come up here—it's too dangerous. I don't want anyone getting hurt. This is only about me."

"Not anymore, chickadee. We are behind you all the way." Evelyn put her arm around Grace.

Looking around at these people she'd come to care for in such a short time, Grace couldn't imagine any of them getting hurt because of her. She shook her head. It seemed ludicrous that any of them would be anywhere near Jason and his anger.

"See what I mean? Everything always gets crazy with a full moon," Evelyn said with a wink to ease the tension.

Canoeing away from Moose Bay toward the Painted Cliffs, they were a solemn group but one more unified with purpose. Even with Psycho Cop after her, Grace hadn't felt this safe in quite some time. She worried, though, about what Jason might do. The group here didn't seem to understand that they should be worried. They didn't seem to be concerned for their own safety. But they should be. Jason had a gun, and that, combined with his temper, was a dangerous thing. Anything could happen to any of them, and she prayed that nothing would. They had families who needed them. And there was no one who needed Grace.

Was saving her really worth their safety? The world needed Nicki's paintings, Kat's poetry, Jake's music, Margot's photographs, Evelyn's art, Jim's knowledge, and Cam's protection. They made the world a more beautiful place to live in. They would impact others in ways they don't even realize.

Louis and Cody too, perhaps them most of all, because they help people get back in touch with not only nature, but themselves. They provide an opportunity for their spirits to become whole again.

Grace closed her eyes and said a little prayer for this wonderful group of people. She prayed for their safety, for their gifts, and that they would be able to continue to share them with the world.

Louis began speaking loudly in a deep, booming voice so that everyone could hear. "There are legends tied to the Painted Cliffs. The images that have been put on the cliff face are called pictographs. They were painted with red ochre, as well as black, white, and yellow dye. The pictographs represent some of Canada's oldest art. The purpose of the images is to summon 'helping spirits' and is tied to shamanism." He shifted in his seat to make sure he could see everyone. "Along with becoming experienced with healing and prophesy, a shaman also must participate in a vision quest. They say that a vision quest is used as an initiation in some Native American cultures. It allows one to find oneself and helps to point them in the direction their life should go."

They paddled in silence, absorbing the information.

"The current will pick up as we round this next bend," Cody called to the group. "See there?" He pointed across a marsh toward some trees. "If you look between those trees, you can make out the cliffs in the distance. You can't see it from here, but just below the cliffs is where the northeast and the northwest rivers merge. It creates huge waves that we call *the gorge*. They're pretty tough to maneuver. By August, you can jump from the cliffs at one of three levels, but in the spring and early summer, we don't recommend it, even with a life jacket. The current is just too strong. Regardless of when, once you jump, you need to swim hard to the side, or you'll be swept into the middle of the river." Picking up the paddle, he leaned out and took a quick little stroke to keep the canoe straight. "It's roughest there, and the strength of the turbulent flow could pull you down to the bottom of the river. You'll pop up about fifty feet downstream, but depending on how long you can hold your breath will determine how you'll do."

"Not my idea of fun," Nicki stated. "So, how will we get a better look at the cliffs?"

"We actually have to come at them downstream and around on the other side of that land mass. We climb up and view them from above. If you're up for a bit of a hike, there are steep trails that let you climb down to the various levels that you would normally jump from. Instead, you can just take a look and come back up when you've seen enough."

The trip would be a distraction while they waited to hear back from Jim's contacts. She hoped they could get in touch with the outfitters soon too. The more eyes on the lookout for Jason, the better.

"We will be crossing downstream about a mile past the gorge. It isn't dangerous, but you need to paddle hard to get to the other side, or you'll be taken downstream and will have to go the longer way to get back up to our route," Cody explained.

About ten minutes later, they arrived downstream of the cliffs and pulled their canoes to a shallow area off to the side. They watched as Cody took his canoe across first with Margot. He angled the bow upstream, and the boat immediately began moving downstream. He managed to keep the angle of the boat, steering as he stroked hard.

Grace watched the paddle as it entered the water in order to memorize his technique and attempt to emulate it when her turn came. His timing was quick and efficient. The arc of the stroke was key to keeping the boat moving forward on the right path. They made it to the other side about fifty feet downstream. He hopped out of the canoe and tied it to a tree on the opposite shore.

Louis raised his voice to ensure everyone could hear as they battled the current by back-paddling to stay in place. "Cody will throw out a rope to you when you get a little closer to the other side. The person in front should set their paddle across the bow in front of them, hold on to it with one hand, and grab the rope with the other while the person in the back continues to paddle and steer." Louis mimed out his instructions. "If you miss that rope, let it be. Pick up your paddle, and we'll come get you downstream."

Raring to give it a try, Grace said, "Ready, Nicki?"

"You betcha!" She leaned forward, elbow up with her paddle poised and ready to go.

Angling the nose of the boat upstream, Grace said, "Let's go!" As Nicki dipped her paddle in the water, with a strong back and good posture, Grace matched her stroke for stroke on the other side. It was a strange sensation as the current propelled them sideways. As Grace pushed her stroke out to get their nose upstream, she disrupted the tempo, which Nicki immediately felt. She hesitated, but Grace called out encouragement.

"We're good. Stroke! Stroke!" Grace wanted to get their timing back. "That's it, nice and quick. Strong pulls. Good job."

Before she could count to ten, Nicki was catching the rope and they were being pulled to the other side. Nicki and Grace were whooping it up and laughing at their success. Grinning from ear to ear, they looked back across the river to see who would come next.

Kat and Jake were just taking their first strokes from the other side. Lean and young, they were physically up for the challenge, just unpracticed and used to moving at a different pace. They weren't past center when they approached, but with a valiant effort on Jake's part, he pushed the canoe close enough just in time. Overpowering Kat's strokes, they ended up coming in backward, so he had to lean out in order to get the rope.

"Damn, you two made it look too easy." He scowled at Nicki and Grace as he pulled the canoe toward shore, walking up the rope hand over hand. They turned to give each other a cocky high five.

Jim and Evelyn were next, and Grace must have felt as nervous as they did. They made a good effort, but it was clear their strokes weren't quick or clean enough to make it across in time.

Louis called out from the other side, "No worries, guys, just take it downstream. Cross when you can—we're right behind you." He and Cam took long, sure strokes to follow downstream behind them. They caught up just past those gathered on the opposite shore and followed alongside them using their canoe to nudge Jim and Evelyn's toward land. The current lessened, and they easily turned in downstream into a little inlet.

"Okay, they'll be fine," Cody said in a reassuring tone. "We'll portage to the other side and meet up with them over there. They'll be awhile, but it'll be a scenic route for them."

As they put on their backpacks and lifted the canoes overhead for the seven-hundred-foot portage, Kat struggled to extend her arms fully. "I hate carrying these canoes. I would have rather taken the longer route." She stumbled as she tried to find a comfortable position.

Walking behind her, Grace could see why. Jake was a good ten inches taller than Kat, so she would be bearing most of the weight of that boat.

"Let me know if you need a break, Kat," Grace said. "I am more than happy to put this canoe down for a minute."

"Sure, sure," she called back over her shoulder. "I've seen those muscles of yours. Looks like you've been training for this trip for a while."

Grace remembered when she had first showed up at the rowing club. She was amazed at how fit they all were. Even more amazing, though, was how some of those whom she had thought were already in great shape would show up the next spring looking like superheroes after a winter of training at the gym with weights, supplementing the indoor rowing machine training. Grace hadn't been on the water for a while, but she had continued what she'd known by doing the winter training year-round. It gave her some feeling of control, but mostly it was a way to alleviate the stress she felt whenever *he* was around. Grace shook away the thought before the fear of whether he'd managed to track her could sink in.

Still, she wondered what was happening with Jim's OPP contacts. Hopefully, the outfitters could give them a warning if someone showed up asking about Dumais Lodge.

Grace put her worries into pushing through the portage. They took a short break just past halfway to let the blood flow back down their arms and into their hands. Then, once their heart rates had come down a little, they picked up their canoes and pushed through to the end.

They popped out of the shadowed trail onto a sun-filled beach overlooking a clear, cool lake, one of the many carved out by the retreating glaciers of the last ice age. Margot pulled out her camera and snapped a few pictures. Grace wished she could do the same.

"I would love to do a bit of sketching here if I could," Nicki said.

Cody turned away from the lake to face her. "Sure. Let's split up for a bit while we're waiting for the others." He saw that Jake and Kat had set down their canoe and were walking along the beach, hand in hand. Turning his attention back to the ladies, he said, "If you want to hang out here, you can. Others may want to paddle up the shoreline to that grouping of yellow birch over there. There's a spot to park your canoe, and you can follow the path to the top of the cliff. The path to the left is shorter. It loops around in a circle, so you can't get lost."

Everyone seemed content to stay where they were to recover. Grace, on the other hand, was just warming up.

"Can I go on my own?" she asked.

"Well, normally, I would say it isn't a good idea, but you're comfortable in a boat and we can certainly bring Nicki with us when she's ready to go," Cody said. "I would come with you except I was going to start a fire and make a snack for us. We brought some tea and bannock with butter and jam." He pulled a container out of his bag and, removing the lid, showed them the flat, round, unsweetened cakes that were made with wheat flour.

Margot clapped her hands. "That looks wonderful! I thought I could smell yeast in the canoe." And as Margot continued to ask what he put in the recipe and whether he would be cooking the bread on a hot stone or in the wrought iron pan, Grace knew she'd found an opportunity to get away on her own. An introvert by nature, she needed time to recharge her batteries when alone. Grace passed Nicki her life jacket but left her paddle in the boat. "You can travel like royalty to the cliffs." Then Grace stepped into the boat with one foot and pushed off with the other.

"Be back in an hour if we don't get there first," Cody called from behind her.

"Sounds good. See you soon," she called back.

Grace paddled away with quick, strong strokes. She was itching to see those painted cliffs, and knowing that she would be the first to view them fulfilled the wanderlust that was at the core of who she was. It was only a short distance to where the shoreline curved to the left. Following it around the bend, she looked for the birch trees and a place to pull in. Peering ahead, she spotted it and made her way there.

But she was no longer alone.

The hair on the back of her neck rose when Grace saw them. They stood looking at her, their faces blank. Something had changed since she'd last seen them.

As Grace paddled slowly toward them, her instincts were screaming to turn the canoe and get out of there. But they hadn't done anything. She told herself that she was being paranoid. Instead, she squared her shoulders and tried to look unruffled.

"Well, fancy meeting you here. I thought you were headed farther north."

"We've already been," Marc replied. "We found the fourth box, and it sent us here." His voice was monotone.

"What's wrong? You both look upset."

"Let's just say his last message kind of creeped us out," Sebastian answered while he pulled her boat onto shore.

"Oh?" Grace prompted, stepping out of the canoe. She straightened, her posture rigid.

Marc passed her the piece of paper. "Take a look."

"4 — The price of anything is the amount of life you exchange for it."

—Henry David Thoreau.

She turned the paper over.

It is time you learned the truth. Be prepared. This is a warning. And a threat.

—X.

Coordinates: 45.5515 N, 78.3700 W

The last set of coordinates had brought them here, and they were clearly upset. No doubt. Their friend, the one they had come searching for, seemed to be turning on them. Why? It hurt and had put them on edge. What was the truth? Why did they need to be warned? How could he threaten them . . . ?

Grace looked deeper into the trees.

"Do you think he could be here somewhere?" she asked.

"I don't think so," Sebastian replied. "Xander was good in the woods, but he wasn't used to living off the land completely. He couldn't have lasted this long on his own."

"What is his game then? Why bring you here just to take off again? Where would he go, back home?"

"He's not home. I would have heard. Cellular coverage is spotty, but I have still been communicating fairly regularly with friends back home." Marc absentmindedly pulled out his phone to check the coverage. "Yeah, it's not great here. Too many trees."

"What are you doing here, anyway?" Sebastian asked gruffly, arms crossed. Grace didn't feel welcome but wasn't going to let him have the pleasure of scaring her away. His charm had faded when she had refused his offer of a drink by the campfire and he realized he wasn't going to get anywhere with her. It had been replaced with what was probably his true nature.

"I came to check out the cliffs. The others are painting and waiting for a couple of boats that didn't make it across the current."

"Oh, so no one is coming with you?" Sebastian gave a quick tip of the head.

"No . . . but the others will be there soon," she hedged, suddenly feeling vulnerable.

Sebastian nodded slowly, processing that bit of information.

He was acting strangely. Warning bells sounded in Grace's subconscious.

"Well, I'm told there's really only one path on this island. It runs in a circle from the beach to the cliffs and back again. The path to the left is supposed to be quicker to the cliffs," Grace explained, hoping to distract him from his thoughts. "Which way are you heading?"

"That's the way we're headed too, I think," Marc said, playing with his GPS.

Heart pounding, Grace kept her face blank. She hoped she wouldn't regret not turning back to the beach. She tied up her canoe, tightened the straps of her backpack, and said, "Okay, I guess we are going the same way."

Marc led the way, and Sebastian brought up the rear. He was prickly today. Hungry and tired, he was probably wishing this "treasure hunt" was over. They walked in silence while Grace reran the words of Xander's note through her mind. *"It is time you learned the truth. Be prepared. This is a warning. And a threat." What is the truth he wants to reveal, and how is he going to do it? A warning and a threat. Why would he warn and threaten at the same time? A threat to one, a warning to the other, maybe? Again, did he know it would be Marc and Sebastian who would come looking for him? It sounded like Sebastian was the only one he let know before he left and maybe he figured he'd ask Marc along.*

His note reminded Grace of her own goodbye letter. It had been shorter. She hadn't had the luxury of time and wanted to get the heck out of there but couldn't resist throwing the fact that she was leaving in Jason's face. It wasn't the smartest thing to do. Had she left without leaving a message, it would have bought her some time. He might have worried a little. Certainly gone looking and called his friends to help. It would have taken him a day or two to go from worried to angry as no evidence of foul play came to light. And then he would start his methodical hunt for her. The way Grace had done it surely lit the fire of his anger immediately, but it had felt so good to let him know he hadn't broken her. She wanted him to know that even with all his mind games and tricks to turn her loving and trusting nature to his agenda, Grace still had a mind of her own. He thought her weak and simple. Grace needed him to know that she was stronger than he thought. She had been biding her time, waiting to find the right moment to go.

On the table Grace had left a white piece of paper she'd ripped from the notepad by the phone. It read, "You thought you could control me. You were wrong." It wasn't much, but she knew it would mess with his head just the same. He wouldn't like being told he was wrong.

Well, Xander seemed to be messing with *their* heads now—Sebastian's for sure. Grace could feel the anger and anxiety rolling off him as he walked.

"What did Xander leave with the note this time?" Grace watched the ground in front of her as she walked.

"Cocaine," Marc answered.

Grace frowned. "How does that affect a person?" She pushed her lips together and felt the flush that started in her neck race to her cheeks.

"People get a big high, then crash and experience emotions that are the extreme opposite. They are depressed, edgy, and often can't eat or sleep properly," Sebastian said.

They walked in silence.

Grace wondered who was carrying that zombie drug, Devil's Breath, now. She assumed Sebastian, and that was dangerous. Her instincts warned her to be careful, and she knew Marc was at risk too. She glanced at Marc's water bottle and hoped he'd been keeping an eye on it. Sebastian could have easily added some powder to it. Sebastian was only worried about his own neck. So why had he come looking for Xander in the first place? He didn't need to. It would have been reasonable to just report the disappearance and let the police investigate.

Now Marc, on the other hand, yes, Grace understood that he would want to look for his friend. He would easily be convinced to come on this search. The opposite was not true. He could not have convinced Sebastian if he hadn't wanted to come himself. What does Sebastian *get* out of this? Why does—

Grace walked straight into Marc's back.

She felt the tension in the stiffness of his muscles. "No," was all he said.

Sebastian skidded to a stop behind them. "What's up?"

Grace and Sebastian stepped around Marc and, recoiling, a shaky hand flew to Grace's mouth.

CHAPTER 14

I Am Invulnerable

—Henry David Thoreau

I T WAS A MAN. IT *WAS* A MAN. NOW IT WAS JUST HIS body . . . rotting. Grace closed her eyes and spun away before vomiting. There were ravens scavenging what was left.

"Get away!" Marc screamed and madly grabbed a handful of dirt and gravel and threw it at them. It was enough to keep them away for a while. One raven with a gray beak—the others had black—flew a few feet out of range, and observed.

"What the . . ." Sebastian stumbled backward.

They stared, taking in the scene before them, carefully trying not to look at the face. The body lay on its back with its arms to its sides. He was fully clothed and looked as though he had lain down in the clearing for a rest. He didn't appear to be hurt; in fact, it looked as though he was lying in a bed of sorts. Rocks had been piled around him. Who had put them there? The murderer? Grace looked behind her and into the trees surrounding them.

She began to speak, then paused, lowered her voice, and addressed Marc. "Is this Xander?"

"Y-Yes, it's him." Marc blinked his eyes, nodding vigorously. "Those are his boots, his clothes his . . . hair."

"I wonder what happened." Grimacing, Grace held her sleeve to her nose as she peered at the body from a safe distance. She couldn't see any obvious signs of trauma beyond the damage the birds had done. Grace continued to focus on small portions of the scene, one at a time, repeatedly fighting the urge to gag. Shaking her head, she said, "I don't see anything wrong with him."

"What—aside from the fact that he's dead?" Sebastian snapped.

Ignoring him, she leaned toward Xander's body as she continued to examine it. "He seems at peace . . . as though he had been prepared for death."

Lifting her head, she saw that Sebastian was bent over holding his knees. Marc was sitting on the ground, staring into space.

To give them time to absorb the shock, she took a step closer, careful not to get too close. What was under his hand? It looked like a soft-sided notebook of some sort. Maybe a novel or a journal. If it was a journal, it might explain some things. Grace looked over and saw Sebastian was staring at it too. Then a thought occurred to her. "Hey. What about the geocache coordinates? Is this the spot?"

Marc, relieved to have a distraction, pulled out his GPS. "Yes, it is."

Looking for the box, she turned away from the body to search the area in the immediate vicinity, slowly moving farther and farther away from it.

"Maybe he didn't get a chance to place the box." Sebastian held his breath.

Grace frowned. "Well, I hope he did."

"Why?" Sebastian sneered, voice raised as his head spun toward her.

"Why not?" Grace countered, nostrils flared, chin high.

"Well . . . well, I don't want to see what's in the box," Sebastian shouted, running his hands through his hair. "It'll be worse than the Devil's Breath, I'd bet."

"Well, I do." Grace shrugged. "We might get answers. Maybe we'll figure out what he was trying to warn you about."

Arms held wide and chin jutting forward, Sebastian said, "Yeah, but he was also threatening us. What if there's something in that box . . . ? I don't want to open it if we find it." Sebastian muttered. "Maybe he got what he deserved."

Grace's heart started to race.

With a rapid intake of breath, Marc blinked rapidly. "How can you say that?" Shoulders back, he flexed his hands—the first sign of aggression she'd ever seen from him.

"Well, you know Xander." Sebastian backpedaled as he held his hands up, palms out. "He always lived on the edge. Always thought he was better than everyone else. He was always bragging about all the different drugs he'd used, and how he was immune to them all."

"Well, he *did* seem immune to them. He never seemed out of control and never got hooked on anything." Marc paused. "He was your best customer."

Grace's eyes widened.

Sebastian looked at her with a smirk. "Does that shock you, princess? We didn't all grow up in a bubble."

196

"This isn't about me," she shot back.

Staring at Marc, he snorted. "Yeah, he was my best customer, and for that reason, I would be the one to know that he was definitely affected by the drugs. He came back for more and more. Couldn't stop. Always paid so, yes, he was a good customer, but no, he wasn't immune."

"I don't believe it," Marc barked. "He was always fine when I saw him. He didn't seem to be *addicted* to anything." He continued trying to think of a situation where he might have misread him.

"Not cool. Why didn't you help him?" Grace stared at Sebastian through narrowed eyes.

"I did. I gave him what he asked for."

"That's not a friend."

"Didn't say I was."

Marc was stunned. "Then who is your friend? Am I? Why'd you even come to look for him if that's how you feel?" he said.

Sebastian gazed past Marc's shoulder with an unfocused look. "I had my reasons."

"Hm." Marc peered at him with new understanding and stood slowly, his skin mottled and eyes hard. "I'm sure you did."

There was a standoff as the big man faced the tall, wiry one, standing on the other side of the body. Then, with startling speed, Marc ran at the body and yanked the book out from under Xander's stiff hand. They heard a sickening crack.

Sebastian stood as if stuck to the spot, not knowing what to do. Deciding that there was no need to do anything at this point, he waited for Marc to make the next move.

Careful not to touch the book more than he had to, Marc opened it to the first page. "It's a journal," he confirmed. "His name is on the inside cover."

Sebastian walked over and casually asked to see it as he grabbed at the corner of the book in an attempt to pull it out of Marc's hands. But Marc was ready, primed with adrenaline, he turned his back on Sebastian and took a couple of steps to create some separation. He'd felt the turning of the tides and realized he was on his own. He no longer trusted him.

"It starts last January. The journal was a Christmas present from Anne." He glanced at Grace. "His girlfriend at the time."

Flipping through the pages, he relayed that it was typical school stuff. He wrote now and again, nothing too consistent. There were breaks before exam time and the odd panicked entry when he was trying to calm himself down. There were references to parties and get-togethers and how Xander had a "magic formula" that always helped him catch up on his studies.

Marc read aloud, "April twenty-ninth says, 'I royally screwed up. Dad's gonna kill me.'" He turned the page. "April thirtieth says, 'Went to get hooked up at S-man's place and came across a situation. Gotta clear town.'" Marc's voice slowed, and his eyebrows scrunched together. "'Not sure he'll let me get away with what I saw.'"

His eyes flickered to Sebastian. Grace stiffened, the hair on her body rising in fear. Sebastian's eyes held hers as he bent to grab a rock from those that encircled Xander's body. Just as she realized what he was doing, Marc said, "What did he mean by that?"

Grace screamed, "Watch out!" as the rock went hurtling toward Marc's head.

She turned to run as Sebastian's long arm lunged at her. Marc tackled him from behind and yelled, "Go!"

Her senses heightened, Grace was aware of everything around her. Her mind worked quickly as she ran up the path, thinking that would be the best odds of escape. Behind her, Grace heard a horrific thud of rock on skull, and she stopped short. Turning, she saw Marc slumped on the ground. Stunned, Grace felt the world fall away as she observed him lying there. Instinct pulled her forward to help but knowing that she could be next, she turned and ran with a surge of adrenaline up the path toward the cliffs. Running through the brush for the most direct route, she felt the sting on her skin from the abuse of branches and shrubs.

Bursting out from the trees into a clearing, Grace had to pull up short in order to avoid going over the edge. Looking down at the wild river below and downstream to where the two channels met, she saw the gorge. When Cody had described it earlier, she couldn't wait to see it for herself, certain it would be peaceful and mesmerizing. Now, knowing she'd soon be in the middle of it, peaceful and mesmerizing weren't words she would use to describe it.

"You don't want to do that," Sebastian warned from behind her.

"I don't think I have much of a choice." Grace kept her eyes on the water. She refused to face him. She didn't have much time before Sebastian knocked her cold and threw her in the river. *Jason'll be pissed he didn't get to do it himself,* Grace thought, with macabre humor.

"Well, that's not true. I figure you have three choices." Sebastian was eerily quiet for a moment. "You jump, you drown. You fight me, you die." He lifted the bloodied rock in his hand. "Or you help me *take care* of Marc, and we live happily ever after."

She heard his footsteps crunch on dried leaves behind her. He was closer now.

"Hey, maybe we can even take care of Psycho Cop together," Sebastian teased maliciously.

Her mouth went dry. She was sure she hadn't spoken about Jason in front of Sebastian or Marc. Her journal *had* been moved. *And he had read it.*

She seethed at the invasion of her privacy. Keeping her back to Sebastian, she turned her head ever so slightly to the left. She could see him in her periphery. His chest heaved, and he reminded her of a wild animal. A predator.

She weighed her options. Grace would never intentionally hurt someone—Marc, Jason, or Sebastian—and although she could live with herself if she killed Sebastian in self-defense, she knew she couldn't overpower him, and she knew he wasn't going to let her live regardless of what he said. Jumping in the river seemed to be the best option.

Grace sprinted forward and jumped with all the confidence she could muster. She did not allow herself to scream on the way down. She wouldn't give him the satisfaction.

She plummeted like a bullet and plunged deep into the rushing water, the powerful current immediately pulling her down. Surfacing, Grace took a big breath and forced her face into the water. Kicking with all her might, she hoped to get far enough out that if he jumped in after her, the current would take them in two different directions.

The waves were at least two to three feet above Grace's head. She made a valiant attempt to swim up the waves and keep her head above water, but as wave after wave came, she tired and was pulled to the center of the river. There, the churning waters flipped her backward. Sebastian stood at the edge of the cliff watching. She saw his smirk as a wave crashed over her. She realized she could no longer time her breath with the waves and was unable to get the air she needed before the next one hit. Grace tried to stay calm, but as the waves engulfed her face over and over again, she screamed for help with the little air she had left in the hopes that someone, anyone, would be there to pull her out if she lost consciousness.

The water dragged Grace to where the rivers merged, and the waves came from both the left and right. She prayed the current wouldn't pull her down to the bottom of the river as Cody had said it could. Time slowed as she awaited her fate. She thanked God when the current pushed her to the right of center, and she wasn't dragged under.

Grace gasped for air and blinked to clear her eyes. Glancing up, she saw Sebastian standing rigidly at the edge of the cliff, watching her. He gazed farther downstream, and she wondered if he would come after her. Grace knew she had better get back to the group before Sebastian caught up with her, and she needed to find them to get help for Marc. Poor Marc. *Sebastian might decide to go finish him off right now!*

Without hesitation, Grace screamed "Come and get me, jackass!" just as she was spun around again by the rush of water. She struggled to turn back to see what Sebastian would do, but when Grace peered back up, he was no longer there. Then to the left, she saw a blur of movement and a splash. Damn. It worked. But at least Marc was safe . . . if he was still alive.

Coughing, she treaded water in the fast current. As the waves lessened, she heard another splash behind her. Sebastian was gaining on her. How'd he gotten so close so fast? He must have caught a more direct route along the shore. He was closing the distance.

Swimming hard for the other side of the wild river, Grace hoped that the current would send him down a different path. Her arms felt like lead, and her legs had stopped listening to her.

He was only five or six feet away when he was pulled one way and she the other. Both unlucky, he was pushed toward her friends while Grace drifted farther away. Spent, Grace caught her breath before making her way to the river's edge. She grabbed on to a root to pull herself up the sharp slope of the riverbank, but her arms were too tired. Letting go of the root, Grace allowed the current to carry her farther downstream in the hopes of finding an easier embankment to climb. The current slowed, and Grace reached a basin to the side where the reeds grew. Moving toward the shore, she gained her footing and slogged through the muddy waters to the water's edge.

Grace tried to spot Sebastian but had no idea where he had gone.

Stepping up to firm land from the wave-churned earth of the shoreline, she smelled the muskiness of the fallen aspen, covered in fungi, its leaves decomposing as the waters pulled them with each tug of the current. Moving away from the river, Grace moved through the trembling aspens and sought the concealing protection of the spruce trees farther in. A cool breeze blew through, and she hugged her arms tightly to her chest.

Picking her way through the trees, she heard the high-pitched whistle of an eagle flying high overhead. She made her way downstream alongside the gurgling river, careful to stay hidden in the trees. She knew she had to get to the group before Sebastian got to her. She hastened over fallen tree trunks and ducked under low-lying branches, ignoring the sting of the branches scraping her bare skin. Where possible, she walked on the moss of the forest floor to avoid the crunch of leaves or the snap of a twig.

Stepping around the fresh pellet-shaped deer drop-pings, she jumped when she heard a rustling to her left.

Heart pounding, she stood frozen and slowly moved her head to look. A plump little beaver waddled, its long, flat tail dragging on the ground behind it as it pulled a branch toward the river.

Wanting to see how far she'd gone, she made her way closer to the river's edge and looked to get her bearings, ever aware that Sebastian was still out there somewhere.

The gorge was upstream—she could see its white caps in the distance—and although the waters were still rough at this point, they weren't dangerous. Remembering where they had crossed the river downstream earlier that afternoon, she realized that if she made her way to the other side, she might find the path they portaged through. That was it! That's how she would find her way back to the others.

Grace decided it was now or never; she grabbed hold of a tree trunk and felt where the bark had worn away. Noticing the fur caught in the rough edges of the trees' outermost layer, she realized that a bear had stopped to groom itself on that very tree. It was all the encouragement she needed. She sidestepped down the steep embankment, but her foot slipped on the loose rocks, her ankle turning and buckling under her weight. Falling into the rapidly moving water, pain shot through her.

Pushing her hands out in front of her and sweeping them to the sides as she kicked her legs out behind her, Grace made her way toward the other side of the river. Letting the current do the bulk of the work, she stayed calm and focused as she steered her way through the churning waters. When the land bent away on her right, Grace realized that that was where she and Nicki had crossed in their canoe. Swimming as hard as she could, she aimed for the inlet on the other side where the portage path was.

Only a few feet remained as she watched the path come level with her and quickly move to her left as she continued downstream. With a shake of her head, she paused in frustration before doubling her effort to get to shore. Grabbing hold of a rock, she hung on until she could get her feet under her to push herself up on shore. A bolt of electricity ran up her calf from her ankle as she remembered her slip into the water. Digging in with her left toe, she hauled herself out of the water to the waist. Catching her breath, she wiggled the remaining way up and out onto the hard earth sprinkled with spruce needles.

Lying on her stomach, she rested before pushing to her elbows and looking around. Thick forest lay before her, strangely quiet, as though it had been waiting for her. Rolling to her back, Grace sat up to survey her throbbing foot. Swollen and purple already, she pulled off her sopping running shoe with a grimace. The fluids rushed to protect the injured foot, causing it to swell further. Knowing the cold water would help, she looked right and left to see a way back down, but there was no spot that was easily accessible.

Grace stood carefully, balancing on her left leg. Putting the ball of her right foot to the ground, she tested it with a bit of pressure. Clenching her teeth together, she paused and tried again, this time stepping fully on her right foot to see if she could handle the pain. Unable to support the weight, Grace fell hard on her hip, her elbow scraping the ground.

She let out a howl of pain and frustration, frightening some birds out of a nearby tree.

I guess I will just have to crawl then, she decided, and on all fours, she began making her way through the trees.

As the brush thickened, she was forced to turn in from the river. Knowing it was the key to making sure she kept going in the right direction, she made sure she could hear the roar of the rushing water in the distance. If the sound became too faint, she would change course, even if it meant backtracking and trying another more challenging route.

The sun moved lower in the sky; knees bruised and bleeding, Grace stopped for a rest.

She thought she heard something different as she sat—a beating sound of some sort. Straining to hear, she held her breath, trying to make it out. Not able to figure out what it was, she shook her head and thought she might have imagined it.

In the thick of the forest, the mosquitoes had been relentless. She'd tried to ignore them, and if she kept moving, it helped. But now, sitting, they had found her growing cloud of carbon dioxide, and more and more decided it was time for lunch. Slapping arms, legs, neck, and back, she yelled, "Get away from me!" and started crawly madly to get away from the bloodsucking scourge.

Grace kept moving, trying to find her way to the safety of her friends. She called out from time to time, hoping someone might hear her, not caring at this point if it was Sebastian. But no one came.

Twilight was upon her, and Grace knew she would have to face the possibility of spending the night in the woods. She grabbed a sturdy branch with a sharp point and found a couple of large rocks. She made a pile of smaller rocks that she could use to scare animals away. She knew she wouldn't be able to keep a pack of wolves at bay, so she tried not to think about that.

Grace lowered her chin to her chest and, shoulders slumped, stared at her swollen foot. Her teeth chattered, and she would have loved a fire but was fearful of the attention a fire would attract. Instead, she kept herself warm by ripping up pieces of moss that could act as a blanket. She huddled up into a ball and pulled them on top of her. But even with the extra protection against the cold, Grace couldn't sleep.

The darkness heightened her senses. She heard things that normally she wouldn't notice, she smelled things that she couldn't place, she felt every little bump and rock under her head and body. Grace strained to see into the darkness but only succeeded in seeing monsters that weren't there. Trying to see in the pitch-black of night felt foolish, but not trying seemed equally so.

She thought she heard the snap of a twig or the huff of an animal breathing throughout the night, but the rush of the wind in the trees ensured she didn't hear anything clearly. What may have been a mouse rustling became a moose in her mind.

Grace could have sworn she even heard a whimper at one point. She sat up, unable to ignore it, and nearly jumped out of her skin when the ghostly apparition of a wolf stepped out from behind a tree in the distance. As it approached, she yelled, "Go on, git!" The wolf whined and lowered its head. Baffled, Grace paused, then pushed her head forward, squinting through the dark. "Wolf?" Its tail began to wag as it inched closer to her. "Wolf!" she cried, tears springing to her eyes. Scratching him behind the ears, Wolf settled down at her side, eventually lengthening out to keep her warm.

In the end, exhaustion overtook her, and for better or worse, she slept.

Grace woke to the *caw, caw* of a crow in the early dawn. Eyes dry, she struggled to open them. Her ankle throbbed, and she felt the sting of the scratches as she moved her legs. Lying on her side, she held her breath as she realized there was warmth along the entire length of her back and legs. Scrambling away, she saw that it was a massive, gray, fur-covered animal, looking at her from calm, blue eyes.

Then she remembered.

"Wolf!" Grace held her arms out toward him.

She also realized they were not alone. Tail wagging, Wolf was looking toward the woods to her right. As she turned to see what he was looking at, a chill run down her spine.

A shaggy-haired creature stared back from its crouch, no more than a dozen feet away. As it rose to its full height,

Grace screamed and it jumped back, hands raised in the air. Remembering the navy long johns, she realized it was the same man they'd passed in the canoe the other day. He looked afraid, which made her pause and remind herself that his name was Simon.

Louis had said there was nothing to be afraid of when it came to Simon. "What do you want?" Grace asked, her voice trembling. He didn't answer. Instead, he turned and walked purposefully into the bush. Not able to follow, she called, "Wait!"

Wolf barked a couple of sharp barks, and Simon came back into the small clearing.

Trusting that Simon was who Louis and Cody said he was, she told him, "I'm hurt. It's my ankle."

Nodding, Simon picked up her shoe and helped her to her feet.

Grace slung her arm across Simon's back as he wrapped his around hers and held her at the waist. He reached up to his right shoulder and held her wrist to keep her arm in place. Grace leaned on him with each step. As they made their way through the trees, Wolf would run ahead and return to see how they were doing, only to run on ahead again. At one point, they could hear him barking in the distance. Assuming he wanted them to go that way, they adjusted their course and kept moving forward.

There was smoke in the air, but before she could register what that might mean, they came out of the trees onto a path that looked familiar and she realized it was the one they had portaged across yesterday. Knowing they were getting close, Grace hopped on one leg, supported by Simon, as quickly as she could.

As she rounded a curve, Grace saw something moving toward her on the path ahead. Blinking, she couldn't make out what it was, friend or foe, but it didn't matter. She was weak with exhaustion, having used her energy stores ten times over. Collapsing on the path, Grace accepted whatever fate may come.

CHAPTER 15

It's What You See

—Henry David Thoreau

S LOWLY, THE PIECES OF HER MIND, LIKE THE GEARS OF A clock, snapped into place and ticked again. Grace was able to think beyond the blanket around her, the hard earth beneath her, and the sound of the comforting words she couldn't process. She looked up to see Nicki making her some tea. It smelled of lavender and chamomile. Cam sat close beside her, rubbing her back. Grace leaned into him, and he put his arms around her and held her tightly; it was as if he needed the comfort as much as she did. He smelled good, and Grace didn't resist. It helped. A lot. She hadn't felt so safe in a long time. Grace clutched the blanket to her chest, then yelped.

"What's wrong?" Cam asked.

She studied her hands, turning them over. They were scratched and dirty. From the trees, dirt, and moss. "My hands." Images from the day before flashed through her mind, and the fear came rushing back.

Grace sat upright. "Sebastian!" she shouted. "Where's Sebastian? Where's Marc?" She let the blanket drop as she stood, and, crying out in pain, she hobbled on one foot while tears streamed down her face. "Where is everyone? Are they okay?"

"Shhh." Cam tried to calm her. "It's only Louis, Nicki, and myself who stayed. The others went back to the lodge last night. Simon headed home already too, with Wolf."

Spots danced in front of her eyes. "But . . . but . . . Marc. He might be dead! And Sebastian might try to kill us. Xander is dead!" Grace fought to stay on her feet as her breathing became shallow.

"Yes, we know. Marc's okay. He found us. He came to and met Cam, who was on his way over." Louis spoke with a low voice, his face soft as he put her arm around his shoulder to keep her from falling.

"We don't know where Sebastian is," Nicki said with a pained expression. "We weren't able to find either of you. We looked for hours. The OPP chopper scoured the area too, but the trees were too dense."

That must have been the beating sound she had heard.

"How did they know to come?"

"Jim called. We needed to report Xander's death."

Grace nodded. "Did they find him?"

"Yes, Marc took them over," Nicki said.

"And they did their investigation while the helicopter searched for you and Sebastian," Cam added. "Once it got dark, they said they wouldn't be able to look any longer, so they took Xander's body and said they would keep looking today.

"It was good that Wolf and Simon found you. He knows our route with the tours and often will swing by to see if he can help out. The river can give us trouble." Louis looked up at the sky, gauging the time of day. "Let's start heading back," he suggested. "We can't take care of you properly here, Grace."

With a nod, Grace looked for the boat and said, "Okay, let's get this over with."

This time, Cam and Grace shared a boat. They followed Nicki and Louis and made good time on their return to Thompson Lake. All were quiet as they anticipated what was ahead.

As Grace canoed, she realized that she was a mess after a night in the forest, but she didn't care.

"What happened yesterday?" Grace asked over her shoulder, stealing a glimpse at Cam. She stopped paddling for a moment.

He gazed out over the water but continued to paddle. There was tension in his shoulders, and his eyes sat above dark circles that hadn't been there the day before. "Well," he began, "when Louis, Jim, Evelyn, and I made it back to the beach where the group had been waiting for us, Cody said you'd been gone over an hour and figured you'd be on your way back already." Cam took long, slow strokes as he pulled the paddle through the water.

"We weren't planning on doing any fishing, and Cody had taken care of the food already, so I said I'd continue to the island and make sure you were okay.

"I saw the boats on the beach and was a little worried not knowing who the other canoe belonged to. I figured it was likely Marc and Sebastian, but I wasn't sure. And to be honest, that didn't make me feel any better."

He spoke carefully, and his pause made her turn around again. Grace looked back at him, and he held her gaze. "Marc came out of the trees with his hand pressed to his head. Blood was running down the side of his face, and his hand was covered in it. He told me what had happened and that you and Sebastian were gone. I felt like someone had punched me in the stomach. I didn't know if you were still alive." His eyes misted over. He blinked away tears.

She could see that he cared. About her. She let the warmth of his compassion flood through her and down her tense neck and stiff body to warm her limbs and settle in her heart. Grace felt like its broken pieces had started to mend.

She started to paddle again.

CHAPTER 16

Lives of Quiet Desperation

—Henry David Thoreau

THEY PULLED ONTO SHORE JUST BEFORE LUNCH ON THE sixth day. The original plan had been to leave for the city by ten that morning, but instead, Grace, Nicki, Cam, and Louis were greeted with hugs and expressions of relief as they stepped out of the boats. Marc was there too, standing at the back of the group.

"What are you all still doing here?" Grace asked. "You should have left by now!"

"How the heck could we leave without seeing that you were okay?" Kat said, tears in her eyes.

"And we certainly couldn't leave without saying good-bye." Evelyn watched Grace hobble out of the canoe. "What happened to your ankle?"

Grace waved the question off with a crooked smile. "It's a long story."

"Besides," Jim said, "I don't think anyone can really leave until the investigation is complete. The OPP will be here in the next hour."

"But . . ." Grace wet her lips and lowered her brow. "Sebastian is still out there."

"Hold up. You think that scrawny guy can take us all on? Not a chance." Jake gave a playful wink and a grin. "Besides, I don't have anyone waiting on me back home. Kat?"

"I'm good wherever you are, baby," she agreed, hand on hip.

Margot crossed her arms. "I'm not going anywhere."

"Nicki," Grace pleaded, "don't you need to get back to your family?"

"You know what? They're good. They've gone to visit their grandparents with their dad. I'm fine for another night." She winked at Grace as she offered her arm.

They helped Grace to the campfire that was already burning low. They'd been roasting hot dogs, and Jake started a few more.

While they waited, Grace told them everything from finding Xander's body to Wolf and Simon rescuing her. "Marc, I'm so glad you're okay." Her chin quivered.

"Thanks," he replied, rubbing the side of his nose.

"Marc had the presence of mind to bring the journal back with him." Jim gave Marc a thumbs-up. "If he hadn't, Sebastian could have gone back for it." Marc looked at the others with a small smile. "It contained valuable evidence to tie Sebastian to a murder, as well as the fentanyl crisis that is happening across the province, and country."

"We had to hand it over for the investigation last night, but we had time to look through it before that." Marc folded his hands in front of him. "It started back last January with day-to-day entries of school and to-do lists. After a while, the writing became stranger and more disturbing." Grace nodded, knowing this. "Then at the end of April, a couple of weeks before Xander began his trip, it got interesting."

Jim looked at the group sitting around the fire. "He mentions an encounter at Sebastian's house."

"Marc was reading that to us when we put two and two together," Grace said. "So, I know something happened at Sebastian's—that's why he came after us—but not the details." They were silent, waiting to hear what Jim had to say. Even the breeze stopped blowing to listen in.

Jim raised an eyebrow, his voice heavy. "Xander witnessed Sebastian shooting a client whose girlfriend died from taking a *single* pill of OxyContin." He paused. "That shouldn't have killed her. The reason it did was because it was laced with fentanyl."

A raven settled itself on a nearby treetop. The movement caught Grace's attention. It stared down at her with an unblinking gaze. Its beak was gray . . . just like the one that had been scavenging Xander's body. The hair on her arms stood up on end.

Marc's eyes looked tired. "The journal said the guy was screaming at Sebastian. He had threatened to call the police, and when he slammed Sebastian into a wall, Sebastian shot him. You *could* consider that self-defense, I guess."

"Maybe, but the fact remains that he was selling drugs that were killing people," Jim said.

Another raven joined the first. And then another. *Why?* Grace thought. *There is nothing to scavenge here. Well, except maybe the hot dogs.* Tearing her eyes from the tree, she tried to focus on what Marc was saying.

"In the journal, Xander said taking OxyContin was like playing Russian Roulette. Depending on which pill you take, you may be fine, or you may die," Marc explained, eyes wide as he took a chug from his water bottle. Water dripped down the side of his cheek to his chin. He wiped it with the back of his hand.

"If Xander witnessed the shooting, why would Sebastian let him leave?" Nicki asked, biting a fingernail.

Jim walked the bag of hot dog buns that were on the ground by his feet over to Jake. "He pretended to agree with Sebastian that it was the customer's problem if they got a bad batch." Jim shook his head. "Sebastian gave him a bag of OxyContin on the house to keep him quiet."

"And instead of calling the police, he came up here?" Margot asked. "Why?" She reached into the picnic basket and passed the napkins and ketchup to Grace.

"Xander knew that Sebastian would question why he'd let him go. In fact, according to the journal, he had his suspicions that the pills in the package Sebastian had given him were *all* laced with fentanyl. It was Sebastian's way of taking care of the problem." Jim stretched his legs in front of him and crossed his arms. "But if Xander didn't take the OxyContin pills at all, or did take them and survived, he was sure Sebastian would be by to tie up loose ends."

Jake reached for a napkin from Grace and wrapped it around the bun before pulling the sizzling hot dog off the whittled roasting stick. He held it out to Grace before motioning for another napkin and removing another bun from the bag.

"But he could have gone to the police right then," Margot persisted.

"He could have, but he didn't want to get involved and he was worried that it would harm his Dad's reputation," Jim said. "Sebastian knew that about him, and it was likely why he let him leave at all."

"So . . . Marc, how again did you and Sebastian know to come up here?" Nicki asked.

"He'd emailed Sebastian, said he had some thinking to do and was going to go camping where he and his dad used to always go."

"He knew Sebastian would know where that was, and by doing this, Xander set the stage. I think he just wanted to play with Sebastian a bit," Jim finished.

"Set the stage for what?" Grace blinked rapidly. "What I don't understand is how Xander died."

Grace squeezed some ketchup on her hot dog and squealed when one of the ravens dove for the bag of nearby buns. She swore to herself as she licked ketchup off her arm and noticed the gooey red splotch on her white canvas shoe.

"Git," Cam yelled, chasing the bird away.

She looked to the tree. The gray-beaked raven was still there, watching and listening.

Jim took out his phone, found what he was looking for, tapped the screen, and began to read from a photo that he had taken of Xander's journal:

219

I wanted Sebastian to think he could get away with murder once again. I know him, and the only reason he will come is to finish me off. Except I will save him the trouble. I will play his game of Russian Roulette, knowing that one of the pills will be a fentanyl-laced bullet in the chamber.

"What does that mean—a fentanyl-laced bullet?" Nicki asked.

"It means that one of the pills of OxyContin in the bag that Sebastian had given him could be laced with fentanyl," Cam explained. "And, just like Russian Roulette, you take your chances. With each pull of the trigger or each OxyContin you take, it could be your last."

"He killed himself? But why would he do that?" Nicki held her hands up, her voice increasing in volume.

Jim looked meaningfully at her, then swiped to the next picture on his phone. Holding it away from himself and squinting a little, he continued:

I think I knew when I began this adventure that it would end like this. When I say 'adventure,' I don't mean this trip north. What I mean is the conscious decision to live life the way I have. I had a sense at ten years of age that I wouldn't be your average guy taking the path most traveled. It wasn't who I was.

Jim found the next photograph and made the picture bigger with his thumb and pointer finger.

I wanted to make a difference and live life to the fullest and teach others what I'd learned. Even when it came to drugs. I don't recommend living this way. It isn't noble or smart. I couldn't resist the temptation, but I should have known better.

Jim flipped to the next picture of Xander's journal.

I regret not being able to do more. I really thought that with a law degree I could make a difference, but experimenting has gotten the best of me. I can't walk away anymore. I need a fix just to function. I struggled in school and told Dad I needed some cash to repeat a couple of classes. Instead, I bought more cocaine—more crack to keep me going to the end of exams.

"It goes on to say that his brain was fried and he wouldn't be able to finish school like he'd planned." Marc's shoulders slumped. "He was depressed and couldn't do it anymore."

The raven tilted its head. Grace glared at it, then turned her back to the nosy bird.

"Once you get into the heavy stuff, it can alter the brain so much that it will never be the same." Jim shook his head.

Margot turned toward Marc. "If Xander only contacted Sebastian, how did you get pulled into this?"

"When Sebastian said he was going to look for Xander, I started packing my bags," he answered simply. "Didn't wait for an invitation."

Kat jumped in. "With the first cache message, Sebastian must have realized he had been tricked. He became more and more uneasy with each additional box, knowing he was being led into a trap."

"Then why did he keep going?" Margot shook her head.

Jake stared at the ground, elbows on knees as he listened. "He needed to make sure Xander didn't come back."

"But how did Xander know that the truth would come out in the end?" Grace asked.

"He sent an email to the OPP the day before his death," Jim answered. "They've been searching for him, but it's a huge park." He paused. "Actually, I think he gave them the wrong coordinates. It was one digit off . . . enough to keep them from finding him right away but not so far off that they wouldn't find him at all."

"He could have saved himself and gone directly to them." Jake stretched out his hands wide, then relaxed them.

"But he would have been dragged into it, and he didn't *want* to live anymore. Besides, it would have killed his dad to know that his son was involved with drugs and murder," Marc said with a pained expression.

Nicki threw her hands in the air. "Worse than his son dying?"

"Possibly." Jim gave a quick nod. "The dad is a pretty powerful guy. Having his son known as a druggy and implicated in murder might have been worse to him."

They shook their heads at the thought.

"And there lies the parenting problem that led to this whole mess," Evelyn concluded.

There were some nods and mumbles of agreement.

Something was still bothering Grace. "So, there was no actual box at this last location he led them to?"

"Not that we could find," Cam answered.

"He signed his last note X instead of Xander," Grace said to herself, remembering.

"X marks the spot," Margot remarked.

As that sank in, it all came together. He'd killed himself intentionally. But not before he implicated a drug dealer and murderer. He went out with style. His story will likely be repeated as an urban legend even if his father tries to keep the details quiet. Unfortunately for him, there were quite a few witnesses to tell their version of the story. Grace only hoped that what happened here would be treated as a lesson, not a goal.

There was a sudden rustle and flapping as the large raven flew off, his curiosity satisfied.

"What drug was that again?" Nicki asked, likely thinking of her boys and what she might have to prepare them for in the not-too-distant future.

"It's sold as OxyContin, but the pills have been laced with fentanyl. The drug in the form used for this purpose is lethal enough that an amount the size of a grain of sand can kill. And does." Cam leaned back in his chair and crossed his ankle over his knee.

Jake snorted. "That is messed up."

Margot glanced at Jake. "You're not kidding." Turning her head back to Jim, she asked, "How do the pills get contaminated?"

"There are two theories as to how the fentanyl gets into the OxyContin." Jim held his pointer finger out and tapped it with the pointer of his other hand. "One, because it's a cheaper substance and is used as filler." He clenched his jaw and tapped his second finger. "Or two, because of cross-contamination—the dealers use the same location to prepare more than one drug and aren't careful to clean up in between."

Jim's phone rang just then. He stepped away to take the call. They all watched and listened, hoping to hear something of value. It was strange to hear a phone ring at all, having been so disconnected from the outside world. "Okay, thanks. We'll be ready." Putting his phone away, Jim addressed the group. "That was Ontario Provincial Police Constable David Bradley. He just spotted Jason Kovacs at a gas station on Highway Sixty. He had a pamphlet for Dumais Lodge and was asking for directions."

"He's coming?" Grace paled and jumped out of her seat. She clutched her stomach and backed away from the road.

"He is," Jim confirmed.

"Oh no," she whispered to herself. She spun away, her breath raspy as she tried to get enough air.

"Grace, listen. Bradley and his partner have a head start, and they're hoping to make some ground to get here well before him. They have been thoroughly briefed and are the best we have in these parts."

Grace hugged herself and stared at Jim, speechless. Her brain worked madly through the possibilities. *Should*

I leave? Leave now? Go a different route home? Was there another route? Where is home? What if I meet him on the road? No, that can't happen. How did he find me? It must have been through the bed and breakfast . . .

Evelyn went to Grace, put an arm around her and squeezed her shoulder. Jim gave her a gentle smile. "He can't do anything here—there are too many of us—but he may try to convince you to go home with him." Jim waited until he held her eyes with his. "Grace, if you leave with him, it would be extremely dangerous. We can't do anything for you if you choose to go. You need to know that."

"There is *no reason* to go back to him." Cam's voice caught as he spoke.

"I won't go back," she stated in a monotone voice.

"If you're at all concerned, we can hide you away." He held his breath and waited for her answer.

"Hiding isn't going to solve anything. If I do that, I'll still be on the run. I need this to end. I need him to show his hand so this can be over and I can start living again." Any other outcome looked incredibly bleak.

"We need to be careful with that," Jim cautioned. "But I agree, we need him to do something that will go on record . . ."

"On record? But that's always been the threat! He's always said that I better not do anything to jeopardize his career. I was hoping for maybe a slap on the wrist, enough to tell him he will be the first you look at if anything happens to me."

"Regardless, we need to set him on edge right away." Cam stood and began to pace. "The sooner he gets flustered, the better."

"True," Jim agreed. "However, we may have too many people here to control the situation easily."

Grace walked toward the road, thinking. Turning, she said, "Cody, I think you should be the one to take everyone to a safe place." Her mouth pulled to the side, and she gave a small shrug. "You're the kind of guy who might set Jason off." Grace watched Cody, hoping he wouldn't take offense.

"Again, that may work in our favor, Grace." Cam's tone was gentle.

She cringed. "You don't know how jealous he is! He made me go to a women's-only fitness club and *still* checked up on anyone I happened to mention in conversation." She looked at each and every face standing there, trying to make them understand. "He would put himself between me and any man at the grocery store. H-He saw red if I *accidentally made eye contact with the boy handing me the coffee at Tim Horton's!* If he sees me standing within ten feet of either of you, he is going to lose it!"

"That's what we're counting on," Cam said with a smile.

"I'll say it again." Jake stood, hands in pocket. "There is only one of him."

"True." Cam chuckled. "Jim is right, though. It's not safe for everyone to be here."

"Yes." Jim surveyed the group. "There are too many people. Too many combinations and permutations to consider."

He turned to Louis and Cody. "Is there anywhere they can safely stay until this is over?"

They regarded one another as they contemplated the solution. A look passed from Louis to Cody. "They could stay with Simon until this is over," Cody said, giving his ear a tug.

No one wanted to see the Bush Man again. His expressionless face had stared right through them and still haunted Grace, even though he was now the hero of her story. She had seen that face over and over again last night in the dark, sure either he or Sebastian would find her. She had imagined herself lying in that spot, never to move again.

"Grace, are you okay, honey?" Evelyn asked.

"I told you that he was there this morning when I woke up." Grace looked out toward the lake as she spoke.

Evelyn nodded.

"I kept imagining he was in the woods watching me last night," Grace said, holding her crossed arms tightly to herself.

"He may very well have been," Louis spoke with his deep, calming voice, "but it would have been to stand guard and keep animals away. And if Sebastian had found you, he would have taken care of that for you too." Louis waited until she blinked and looked directly back at him. "He might not be able to communicate well anymore, but he is still a good person."

"Let's do it then," Jim said with a curt nod, then turned to Cody. "How will you get there?"

"We can take the boats. His place is just over there," Cody said, pointing to the other side of the lake.

"Sounds good. Okay, who do we have here? Ev, I need to be a part of this. I'll look out of place at my age without you. Are you game to stay?" he asked, obviously hating to do so.

"Of course, honey. I have a head on my shoulders and hardly look a threat. He won't pay me any mind, don't you worry."

"Okay, that makes two of us, plus, of course, Cody, Grace, and Cam. Margot, are you willing to stay? I'm guessing you've been in some unstable situations before. Your experience might come in handy."

"Thought you'd never ask," she said with a smile and a wink to Grace.

"Okay . . . now that we have that figured out," Louis said with a twinkle in his eye, "I should probably get this group out of here before the cavalry comes."

CHAPTER 17

What Lies within Us

—Henry David Thoreau

T HE CAMP WAS ABUZZ WITH ACTIVITY AS THEY MADE preparations to leave for Simon's cabin. As their bags were already packed for the return trip home, it didn't take long. Louis had his rod and shore lunch tools ready to go, along with a few other necessities needed to feed the group for the day. They were loaded down but prepared to stay the night if they had to.

Grace made her way to the camp kitchen and swung a leg over the bench seat of the picnic table. Straddling it, she watched Kat jump out of the fishing boat and run back to the cabin to get something. A loud slam of the door was followed by Kat running back to the boat with a pillow tucked under her arm. Grace wondered if they *would* be gone overnight.

She didn't know what the day would bring. Would the OPP finish their questioning and give Jason an escort home with a strong warning for him to keep his distance from Grace? She knew that wouldn't be enough. *But what would?*

Grace heard the crunch of gravel and was startled to see Cam appear in the doorway. He stopped mid-step, eyes widening, obviously surprised to see her as well. Heart hammering in response to his unexpected physical presence, she took a deep breath, held it, and let it out slowly.

As he walked toward her, she looked from his face to his chest. Oh, to put her face on his chest and listen to his strong heartbeat with his arms wrapped around her. Again, Grace's mind went back to that dance. She'd put her forehead on his chest as the song had slowed, knowing she would have to walk away when it ended. Such an intimate gesture toward someone she'd just met, but the way he'd pulled her hand to his chest made the motion easy and natural. She'd given in to the moment, knowing it would be more comfortable than to keep the inch or two of space between them. He'd held her close then, telling her he was happy that she had. It also told Grace that he wanted her closer and for longer than the dance. It seemed they had been made for each other. They'd each found their perfect partner in dance and in life.

And as the last notes of the song had played out, they kept dancing. Even when those notes had stopped, they stood, as others had begun to leave. Grace saw the surprise in his eyes at feeling so much so quickly; she felt it too, but she had known she wouldn't dance with him again—she couldn't—and was numb as he had led her off the dance floor. He felt the change in her and said, "We'll have another soon." Grace smiled wistfully, knowing there wouldn't be another. She and Jason had only been dating a few months at that point, but she couldn't live with herself if she acted on a whim. Even asking his name or taking his number or email would feel wrong and ruin that wonderful moment they'd had.

"What?" he questioned, walking closer.

"Oh, I was just thinking back to that dance," Grace admitted.

"That was something else, wasn't it?" he said, looking down at her with a little shake of his head.

"It was. It nearly killed me to walk away that night." Her stomach felt queasy just as it had then.

"I understood." He eased himself onto the picnic table, feet on the bench.

She smiled softly. The memory was always so bittersweet.

"I believe we've been given another chance." He ducked his head. "I know this situation isn't perfect, but they rarely are." He waited until her eyes met his. "This was meant to happen. We'll take care of things with Jason, and when you're ready and if you want me, I'm yours," Cam promised.

"It's too soon to be talking like this," Grace insisted, though her heart didn't believe it. "It isn't right."

Cam let out a small sigh. "All's fair in love and war, Grace."

That's what Evelyn had said, she thought, staring blankly at the ground.

"This will be over soon. The police will get here before him. And it'll all be okay."

He squeezed Grace's hand in encouragement and wondered the same thing she had earlier: *How will they get Jason to let her go?*

Suddenly impatient, he stood and smiled. "I'll be right back."

As he walked away, she admired the view. His broad shoulders wore that blue-and-cream plaid shirt well. His Levi's, well-worn, hugged his hips on a tall, athletic frame. Cam looked perfectly at home in these beautiful surroundings. He fit right in. Grace could see him fitting in her life as well. It would be easy.

And as he walked up to Jim and began discussing something with him, the look on Jim's face, the concentration, the respect, acceptance, or belief in what Cam was telling him confirmed her hopes. Cam was a good guy. Jim would know the difference. Grace's heart lightened, and her head felt giddy with the possibilities.

Grace watched as the rest of the gang shoved off and waved goodbye. As the canoes passed by some loons in the distance, one of the birds called a warning not to get too close to her babies. With that, Grace was brought back to the task at hand. She needed to be mentally prepared, if nothing else. What would happen when Jason Kovacks drove up that road? Where would she be? Where *should* she be? Should she be hidden away and wait for him to ask about her?

Glancing at her watch, it was already 2:40. He could be here at any time. Grace stood, feeling the need to make a more definite plan with Jim. His experience was reassuring.

She found him in the lodge with Cam and Cody sitting in the happy-hour chairs. Marc was sleeping on the couch.

And as she sat down, the spring door to the lodge told her that Margot was joining them as well.

"What's the plan?" Grace asked. "I need to know what to do. What not to do. My opinion is that Jason needs to snap before the police are done with their questioning. They can't leave with him still here."

"We were thinking the same thing, Grace." Jim touched his fingertips together, forming a steeple. "We're just not sure how to do that quite yet."

Just then, Jim's phone buzzed. As he read the text, Evelyn walked into the room from the kitchen with a cup of coffee.

"What does it say?" she asked, walking to his side.

"It's Constable Lyons. She says they just turned onto White Spruce Road."

"Okay, that's their last turn. They'll be here in five." There was tension in Cody's voice.

"And Jason will be right behind them," Cam finished. "Grace, go to your cabin. We'll be here when Jason arrives, and one of us will come get you when it's time.

"Wait at least until they get out and away from their vehicles and we've introduced ourselves. Margot, position yourself in a chair and pretend to read or play with your camera," he continued, setting the scene.

"Will do," she promised.

"Evelyn, Jim, go down to the beach and make like you're coming back from a walk. Cody and I will get our rods and fish off the dock on their arrival. We'll make the scene as natural as possible and watch Jason's reaction to Grace when she comes out of the ladies' cabin."

They took their positions. Grace would need to feign shock at seeing him and pretend to fight the urge to run. She was never much of an actor but figured her natural reaction to him should be sufficient in itself.

A few minutes later, she heard tires on gravel as a vehicle pulled into the drive. Grace looked out the window and saw the two constables getting out of their vehicle. One was a small, blond woman with a long ponytail starting from the base of her neck. The other was a tall, awkward-looking man, but a beast just the same, standing well over six feet tall and poker-straight. He was in his late forties, she about the same. Definitely experienced. They hadn't sent newbies, to her relief.

Grace could hear their muffled introductions. First with Cody, who shook their hands and introduced himself as the owner of the camp. Then with Cam, who strolled up behind him with an easy wave from farther back. Their names were Lyons and Bradley. Bradley and Jim exchanged a look. Jim had said Bradley was his contact—the contact who had been informed of the situation.

Seeing them turn toward the road, her heart began racing, knowing that Jason had arrived. The familiar black jeep rolled in, covered with dust—so unlike its normal perfectly polished finish.

Jason stepped out of his vehicle. Shockingly handsome, he had a strong, straight nose, full mouth, and a square jawline. His hair was dark and perfectly in place, as were his black jeans, T-shirt, and boots. He was unruffled and smooth, with eyes as cool as his demeanor. If he was surprised to see the OPP officers, he didn't show it.

"Hello," Cody welcomed him. "What can we do for you?" Wolf growled quietly at his side.

"I just wanted to check out your lodge. I was thinking about doing a bit of fishing with some friends this summer." Jason stood with his hands stuffed in his pockets. Taking a couple of steps forward, he observed the police officers and scanned the rest of the people mulling about. "What's going on?" he asked, glancing at the police car. "I hope I'm not disturbing you. I can come back later if you need some time." He thumbed back toward his vehicle.

Grace waited, listening.

"No worries." Cody walked toward Jason to shake his hand. "Cody."

"Jason," he replied, returning the handshake firmly.

"I can give you a bit of a tour once we've finished here," Cody offered, nodding toward the constables. "If you'll excuse me. Feel free to look around."

"Are these all your guests?" Constable Lyons asked, observing each one at a time as Cody walked back toward her.

"No, some others have gone fishing, and then there are the two who found the body, Marc Parenteau and Grace Rhodes. He's in the main lodge, and she's having a nap in the women's bunk house at the moment," Cody said.

"They are still looking for the other man, Sebastian Grenier," Jim explained.

"I hope they find him soon," Cody said. "He forced Grace off the Painted Cliffs up by the gorge."

Grace watched Jason's face through the window as victory and fear both played across his face.

"This Grace . . . Is she okay?" Constable Lyons asked, looking up from her notepad.

"Oh, yes, she's fine," Cam answered, standing tall with a gleam in his eye. "We took good care of her."

Grace watched Cam's mannerisms and listened to his words and was gobsmacked. *Your funeral*, she thought to herself. She knew that Jason would be ticked with Cam's familiar tone and seeing red already.

"We will have to speak to her at some point," Lyons stated.

"I'll go wake her," Cam offered with a wink, as Jason ground his teeth together.

Grace waited for Cam to come get her. He knocked and called out with warmth in his voice, "Grace? We've got company." He was doing everything he could to provoke Jason.

She opened the door to see him standing there. Grace could only stare. She quivered from head to toe and struggled to catch her breath. Her heart raced, and he whispered, "It'll be okay."

Grace steeled herself and, with a deep breath, pushed her fears away and pretended she was relieved that the authorities had come to put closure to the situation. Stepping past Cam, she pulled her damp T-shirt away from her skin and raised her eyes to see who was there.

Time slowed as she saw Jim and Evelyn watching her from a distance. Margot sat in an Adirondack chair and gave her a small smile. Cody looked at her with serious eyes. She made eye contact with the female police officer, then the male.

With her next step, Grace stopped cold as she looked at that face she'd come to hate. She must have been a better actress than she thought, thinking back to all those days, weeks, and months that she needed him to believe she still cared so he wouldn't punish her with further restrictions to her freedom. The problem was, a small part of her did still care, then and now. But Grace was sick of living in fear, under his control, with no future. Nothing was worth that.

He stepped forward. "Grace."

His need to prove that he'd known she would be here was worth showing his cards to everyone present and that he wasn't there to book a fishing trip. He didn't care if they knew that she had left him. In his arrogance, he felt he was in control of the situation and that Grace would return to him.

She stepped back instinctively in response, and he froze, evaluating the situation. He looked at the people present, the witnesses. Considering that there were some experienced police constables present, he decided to play it cool.

"Are you okay?" he asked from where he stood.

Grace carefully nodded.

"Do you know this woman?" Constable Lyons asked.

Eyes on Grace, Jason played to his audience. "Yes, she is my *girlfriend*." He cocked his head and stepped toward her, feigning the emotions he had never been fully capable of feeling.

"N-Not anymore." Grace shook her head with short, quick movements.

Jason's eye twitched.

Seeing him brought back a flood of memories, which left her sick to her stomach. His arrogance was huge. Everything was always about him. He needed attention and praise and always felt the need to prove something. He didn't really care about her. Grace was just the prize. A convenience and a means to an end. He needed a woman in his life, not for companionship, but to prove he was a man. What he didn't realize was that a real man didn't threaten or control a woman. A real man cared for and protected her.

She stood very still, sweat dripping down the back of her neck. "How did you find me?" She had to know.

"I tracked your phone." He smirked, tossing it to her.

Grace's voice rose in frustration. "But I removed the SIM card!"

Jason laughed. "That doesn't do anything. I had the IMEI number from your phone. I just needed to write up a police report and get assistance from the network service provider to track your 'lost' phone."

"And you knew my IMEI number *how?*" She already knew the answer. He would have recorded it somewhere on the day he'd given it to her.

He didn't respond, knowing she had already pieced it together.

"And you found the pamphlet in the lobby, the artists' retreat left on Tuesday, and you figured you'd follow the lead . . ." she finished for him.

"Bingo." Jason was smug as he stood feet apart, arms crossed. "I called to see if there was room in the next trip." He chuckled and looked to Cody. "And was told that they meet up at The Lieutenant's Pump. I stopped there, showed the bartender your picture, and he said you'd left with the group that heads up north for the week."

Grace closed her eyes while she let that all settle in.

"Grace, may I speak with you for a minute?" Constable Bradley stepped toward her and spoke with a deep, booming voice. To Cody, he said, "Is there somewhere that she and I can speak in private?"

Cody led them toward the lodge while the others stared at Jason with open hostility.

"Jason," Lyons began, eyebrow raised, "why is it that you needed to track Grace down?"

"She took off," Jason said. "I wanted to make sure she was all right."

"Uh-huh." Constable Lyons flipped her notepad closed. "I'll be in touch."

And so, not being able to do anything else at the moment, Jason Kovacks lazily gazed at Jim, Evelyn, Margot, and Cam, who were making their way to the lodge, then through the trees to the lake. "Mind if I take a look around?" Not waiting for an answer, he sauntered down to the water.

Grace stood tall while they walked to the lodge but as soon as they were out of sight, she crumpled and would have fallen if Cody hadn't caught her. He and Bradley moved her to the nearest chair. Evelyn bustled into the room and, seeing Grace, promised to be right back with a glass of water.

Margot found a nearby chair and sat tall, shoulders back. She was pissed; Grace could feel the waves of anger rolling off her. Her anger strengthened Grace. Even with Jason so close, she felt stronger with their support.

She waited for Bradley to speak.

"Grace." Bradley stood, hands on hips. "I really just wanted to give you some distance from Jason and given . . . your support system . . ." He observed the room. "I believe we can speak freely here."

Lyons stepped into the room. Eyes on Grace, he continued.

"Jim has apprised us of the danger you're in. We don't take that lightly, but, first, we're going to need to question you and the others with regard to Alexander Fortin and what you observed when the body was found." He paused to let her take a sip of her water.

Cody addressed the officers. "Where would you like to start?"

"Let's get some questions answered," Constable Bradley suggested. "We can start with Monsieur Parenteau."

Constable Lyons made her way to stand beside her partner. "Until then, there is safety in numbers, so make sure you don't find yourself alone with Jason. Keep your distance."

As Grace followed Cam back outside to await her turn for questioning, her mind raced through the possibilities of what was to come. Once the police had finished with the questioning, would they go? Would Jason leave with them? If Jason couldn't get her on his side, she was a threat to his career and needed to be eliminated. He might play it cool while he was here, but he would be making sure she didn't talk afterward. Grace couldn't live with that hanging over her. She needed him to threaten her in front of witnesses so that he couldn't touch her later.

Speak of the devil . . . she jerked her head back as she saw Jason making his way to the lodge from his truck with a bottle of rye in his hand. *The nerve of the man! He just shows up here and starts drinking?*

Grace waited until he was safely inside the building before she looked up at Cam. "What do I have to do?"

Cam paused for a moment. Then he nodded.

"We need him to show intent to harm. Without it, he will get off with a warning. The problem is, it's risky. Regardless, Grace, if it's okay with you, I would like to push this guy."

"How?" she asked.

"By being at your side. Standing a little too close for his liking. Putting a hand on your back. Making eye contact with you that lasts longer than your average glance. Make him jealous, make him fume. He'll want to lash out."

"What should *I* do?" she asked, her heart racing. She couldn't imagine Cam doing any of that in front of Jason.

Grace hadn't been allowed to interact with other men in any social setting for so long that she truly didn't know how he would handle it.

"Just be yourself. React normally given the fact that he's here. If you feel you shouldn't be talking to me because it will make him mad, walk away from me if you want. It will be my job to get him on his heels."

And just as Cam said the words, standing close and looking down at her, Jason came out of the lodge holding a red Solo cup in one hand and his bottle of rye in the other.

He took in the situation, body rigid, nostrils flared. The intimacy of the conversation had set him off. Not only was she speaking to another man, but she was speaking to one who was every bit his match physically.

Grace blanched, and as she started to walk away, Jason kept his anger tightly reined and said with a sly smirk, "They said they are ready to talk to you, Grace. Apparently 'Monsieur Parenteau,'" he said, using air quotes, "thought he should shower before being questioned." She was still under his control, even here. Grace stared at the ground with vacant eyes. Slowly, she turned, cheeks burning, this time toward Dumais Lodge and Jason.

At home, a conversation with another man would land Grace in deep water later. Jason would have felt the need to belittle her and call her names and suggest things about her intentions that just weren't true. Today, however, he would not get that opportunity. Grace would not be alone with him, and he would not talk to her that way. She was no longer his to mistreat. Grace stood taller, lifted her chin a little in defiance, and looked Jason straight in the eye as she neared him. She was done with his intimidation. Bring what it may, this would end now.

Cam walked closely beside her, and he nodded at Jason as they approached.

Jason stared Cam down. *If looks could kill,* Grace thought as they passed.

Stretching to his full size, Cam returned the look with narrowed eyes and a tight-lipped smile.

CHAPTER 18

The Price of Anything

—Henry David Thoreau

IT WAS LATE AFTERNOON WHEN ALL THE INTERVIEWING was complete. Grace had gone back to her bunkhouse to hide out for a while but had been called back to answer a few additional questions. She was last to finish. Constable Lyons went to let people know that they could return to the lodge.

Constable Bradley excused himself, and Grace leaned back in her chair and let out a breath. She was thankful that they had kept the questions to what had happened from the time they left Dumais Lodge the previous morning to when Grace had made her way back with Louis, Nicki, and Cam.

She had been concerned that the questioning might start with why she had chosen to come on the artists' retreat. Grace didn't want to share those details. They were part of her escape from Jason, and it would have been unfair if she'd had to share them. It was part of her new life. Her new beginning, and it had nothing to do with Sebastian or Xander.

People had started to trickle back in, so Grace stood and wandered over to the kitchen to see if she could help with supper. Louis came in a little flustered and said, "Leftovers it is!" He opened the fridge and dove in, pulling out containers of this and that.

Grace had started pulling the lids off the Tupperware containers when she heard a loud thump and bang. Jason stumbled into the room saying, "Sorry, sorry." The smell of booze was strong, and Bradley guided him into the living room. Grace shook her head. He was a drinker but not usually to this extreme.

Evelyn stopped in the kitchen and said, "A pitcher of water, please." She leaned, straight-armed, on the counter and stared at it, while Grace ran to get her the jug.

Passing it to Evelyn, she whispered, "How much has he had?"

"A lot." Evelyn looked back over her shoulder toward the front room. "He's been at it all afternoon. After his first drink, he has been drinking the rye right from the bottle."

Jason's loud voice carried into the kitchen. "That's just how it is," he said, summing up his opinion on something.

"Why is he still here? I wish he'd just leave," Grace said through gritted teeth.

"He won't be driving home tonight, that's for sure." Evelyn's lips were pinched tight. She knew Grace hadn't wanted him to stay any longer than he needed to.

"I don't know that we should be heading to the city tonight, either." Louis transferred some leftover risotto to a fiery orange cast iron casserole dish. "It's getting late."

Grace groaned.

245

"Don't worry." Louis turned the oven on. "We'll make room for our extra guests. Jason can sleep on the pullout couch in the living room, and Marc can sleep with the guys. I don't know if Lyons or Bradley are staying, but they'll have to sleep in the bunk houses if they do. They have good, solid locks so you can sleep easy."

Looking at the containers on the counter to determine if there would be enough food, Louis grimaced. "I had better pull out that roast beef too. I hope it's still okay to eat."

While the food heated in the oven, they set the table, and when Grace had nothing else to do, she made her way to the front room. There was a lively discussion over what was the best type of beer. Ale, lager, and stout were mentioned, but she didn't plan to give an opinion, so she tucked herself into the corner to listen and stay out of Jason's line of sight.

He slurred his words and laughed at his own jokes. Cam and Cody humored him. Jim and Evelyn sat listening, unable to get a word in edgewise. Margot watched, eyebrow raised as though waiting for things to go south. Lyons and Bradley sat on the other side of the room. Bradley was reading a tattered paperback he must have found in the magazine rack that sat on the floor beside him. Wolf lay on the ground, his head on his paws, one eyebrow raising, then the other as he listened to the raucous.

They were all relieved when Louis called them to the table to eat.

"Well, it's about time!" Jason called out good-naturedly to him. He made his way to the dining room and took the first chair he could find at the end of the table.

Grace tiptoed behind him and went down to the other end of the table.

Jason glanced down the long table at Grace often throughout the meal. His looks reminded her of all the games he'd played before, and here he was trying to do it again. Sickened by him, she focused on her meal and tried to ignore him, but it was too much. There had been just too much emotion today, and she was spent. Grace took another bite of her meal and chewed without tasting.

Cam sat across from Grace in silence and, sensing her mood and thoughts, waited for her to look up. Catching her eye, his stare was intense as he tried to convey that it would be okay, to stay strong.

Feeling that they were being watched, Grace saw Jason glaring at them, livid. Averting her eyes, Grace stared down at her food, knowing she couldn't eat anymore. His eyes were off her, and she peeked over once again to see that his focus had changed to Cam alone. Grace felt a ripple of fear down her neck. She looked at Cam, and the tension in his body indicated that he felt it too. But instead of staring him down, he reached across the table and took her hand.

"Grace, are you done with your dinner?" Cam asked.

She nodded.

"You look ready to drop. Do you need to go lie down?" Grace shook her head yes. "Okay, let's go. I'll walk you out," he said, and took her plate.

Grace clumsily pushed her chair back, feeling shy and awkward with everyone's eyes on her. She stood up and walked past the remaining guests, and the end of the table where Jason was sitting.

As Grace walked by him on her way to the back door, he growled, "Where do you think you're going?"

She hesitated, not knowing what to do or say.

"She's going to bed," Cam answered.

"Since when are you in charge of Grace?" Jason redirected his belligerence to Cam.

"I am not in charge of Grace. I am only looking out for her well-being. Look, she's ready to drop of exhaustion." And with those words, Grace felt faint as the reality of that statement sunk in. It had been over twenty-four hours since she had jumped off that cliff and spent a restless night in the woods. She had slept but not deeply.

"Well, if she needs putting to bed, I'll be the man to do it." Jason stood up, knocking the table and spilling a glass of water.

Grace stepped back in fear knowing what his intention would be with that statement. More than once, he'd forced himself on her after a few too many.

With that, Cam lost his cool. "You will not go near her. You don't have a claim on her. She's not yours." Cam put himself between Grace and Jason.

"And whose is she, do you think?" Jason leaned forward. "Yours?"

"No. She's no one's. She's her own person and needs to be left the hell alone."

Jason lunged at Cam, tackling him at his waist, knocking him into the wall. A picture frame fell to the ground, and the glass shattered. Grace was bumped hard and would have fallen if Cody hadn't reached out and grabbed her arm and back.

They crashed to the floor, and Jason was able to pin Cam on his back. Straddling him, Jason got a few solid punches in before Cam managed to roll out from under him, grab his wrist, and twist his arm, shoving it up his back. Face-first on the ground, Jason struggled to free himself, but Cam forced his shoulder down with the other hand, ensuring he had no leverage.

He held him there until Jason calmed down and stopped struggling.

"Okay, okay. Sorry." He swallowed and caught his breath. "I shouldn't have done that." Jason relaxed his muscles and conceded the fight. Cam let go of his arm and stepped back, chest heaving.

Once released, Jason stood slowly, hands in the air, his face slack. From under furrowed brows, his eyes shot daggers at Grace. He turned away, closed his eyes, and gave his head a small shake. Opening them again, he scoffed and looked at her with utter disbelief. Then, before they realized what was happening, he had grabbed a steak knife off the table and spun to hold Grace in front of him. He held one arm across her front, pinning both her arms and held the knife to her throat with the other hand. Glaring at the others, he yelled at them, "Get back!"

Cam stood, arms and legs wide, and tried to figure out what he could do. Lyons's chair crashed backward as she jumped to her feet. Evelyn screamed. Bradley already had his gun at the ready.

Grace was sick. Jason panted in her ear, and with each exhale, the reek of alcohol was strong in her nose. His arms were like a vice, forcing her to take shallow breaths. The blade of the knife pressed hard into her neck, cold against her hot skin. Her neck stung, and she felt something trickle down her throat and onto her breast.

This was no less than she had expected to happen at some point. She just hadn't expected the audience. And for as much as Grace didn't like being the center of attention, she was glad. He wouldn't get away with it. She might die, but he would go to jail and wouldn't terrorize another woman again.

She knew what she needed to do to survive. She needed to go limp and soft and pretend to feel regret for whatever had set him off. He would immediately feel the difference in her. Grace had done it so many times before to diffuse him. He would sense it, lower the knife, and she would turn to look him in the eyes with love. It would be a distraction. Enough of one that they would get the knife away from him, and she would live.

It had worked in the past . . . but, perhaps not today. Today was different. Things had changed.

Regardless, Grace couldn't, she wouldn't. She was done with pretending.

Grace looked at Cam and said, "I'm sorry, I can't do this anymore." She closed her eyes, waiting for the pain she knew was on its way.

Cam shouted, "Grace, no!"

Grace felt Jason's body tense as he heard her betrayal; she no longer loved him and was no longer controlled by him. His elbow raised as he began to pull the knife across her throat, and as Grace resigned herself to the end, she heard a bang and felt a warm splatter against her cheek. She felt herself being pulled backward as arms grabbed her from the front and kept her from falling. Cam pulled Grace to him and held her as she looked wildly around trying to understand what had happened.

Grace saw two guns raised and trained in her direction. One in the ready, one pointed up with a little smoke rising from it where the kick of the shot had moved it. She looked up from the gun into Bradley's calm and satisfied eyes.

As the guns were slowly lowered, Grace tried to turn to look back at Jason, not sure if the danger had truly passed. Cam held Grace tight in a bone-crushing hug, keeping her from witnessing the aftermath of what had happened. Realizing she didn't want to see, she surrendered to the moment as everything began to sink in.

CHAPTER 19

Give Me Truth

—Henry David Thoreau

THE OPP HAD TAPED OFF THE DINING AREA IN THE lodge and covered Jason's body. The dishes were left as they were.

Cody sent word to Louis, and the other members of the retreat returned by dark. Staring at the fire, Margot filled them in on the events of the afternoon. They were upset at the news but were relieved that they didn't need to spend the night away from camp. They had met their mystery man of the bush, Simon, and spent some time with him in the afternoon. It appeared as though their discomfort with him was, for the most part, gone now that they knew his story and had gotten to know him a little. He had been invited to come for supper but had declined with a shake of his head. He still preferred his own company.

Louis and Cody came out of the lodge carrying two trays of drinks. A helicopter flew overhead, the search for Sebastian done for the day.

"I thought we all needed something a little stronger tonight." Cody made his way around the circle to give each person a glass of bourbon on ice.

"Well, who would have thought the week would go as it did?" Evelyn kept a close eye on Grace.

Not me, Grace thought. This time last week, she had been at home with Jason watching a movie. She'd known she had to get out of there but didn't know if she would be successful.

Sunday had been the turning point. It had been another lonely day, where he had gone to the gym after his second night shift and brought home groceries so she could cook them dinner while he slept. It was a solitary existence without free will. Grace hadn't been herself for a while. She had done and said what was expected, not ever being allowed to voice her opinion, or plan or dream. It was a life where Grace didn't exist.

I can't believe he's dead. Grace stared at the fire.

She took a sip of her drink and shivered as the strong alcohol burned her throat, making its way to warm her belly. No one asked any questions. They spoke quietly of the events and were tactful of what they said. Cam stood guard beside her.

The fire was burning low when Jim came out of the lodge. All eyes turned to him for an update.

"Another team, the Serious Incident Response Team, also known as SIRT, will be coming out to question those of us who were in the lodge . . . for supper," he said, searching for the right words. "I don't know how long they will take to get here, but they promise a twenty-four-hour response time." Jim cleared his throat and held up a tattered book he had been carrying. "I found this in the lodge." Their curiosity was piqued. "It's an old paperback of Henry David Thoreau quotes," he explained, answering one question, raising another.

Grace took another sip of her drink. She didn't really want to think about the geocaching anymore.

"Jim, I don't really think we need to talk about that right now," Evelyn said softly, looking at Grace.

"No, I understand that." Jim smiled at his wife. "What I thought we might like to do with it is to read our favorite Thoreau passages." He addressed Marc. "Xander, like I, seems to have been a fan, and I thought it might be a good way to honor him." He held the book on its side in order to catch some of the light from the fire. He put his index finger to a page and began to read. "Here it is, one of my favorites: 'Live the life you have imagined.'" His eyes smiled at Grace across the fire, then he passed the book to his left, to Nicki.

She looked for a moment, then read, "'Friends . . . they cherish one another's hopes. They are kind to one another's dreams.'"

Cody took the book next and flipped through the pages with his thumb. "I like this one: 'Many men go fishing for all their lives without knowing that it is not fish they are after.'" Grace hoped he found what he was looking for. He passed the paperback to Louis, pointing at a passage.

Louis smiled and read, "'Heaven is under our feet as well as over our heads.'"

"Isn't that the truth," Margot said, leaning forward to take the book from Louis. "I'll miss it here." She glanced through the quotes, searching for one that spoke to her. "This is a good one for me and Simon both, I think: 'I never found a companion that was so companionable as solitude.'"

They all nodded in agreement. Marc sat next to Margot and, clearing his throat as he read through some options, began, "'The most—'" His voice cracked, and he paused to clear his throat again. Then, he spoke the words: "'The most I can do for my friend is simply be his friend.'" They all were hit by the simplicity of those words but specifically the truth of them, especially here and now.

When he was ready, Marc passed the book to Cam as if he were saying goodbye to his friend. Cam took it slowly, with respect, smiling at Marc as he did. He studied the open page but didn't see what he was looking for there, so he turned the page, running his finger down it. "Here we go: 'It's not what you look at that matters, it's what you see,'" Cam said, reading the words carefully. He turned to Grace, and she realized that he *saw* her for who she really was. She blinked as tears threatened once again. He gave Grace a sideways hug and passed her the book.

Grace spotted hers right away and spoke with confidence. "'Not until we are lost do we begin to find ourselves.'" She lifted her chin and passed the book of quotes to Evelyn, then leaned back in her chair to await Evelyn's choice.

She said, "'What lies behind us and what lies ahead of us are tiny matters compared to what lies within us.'" She reached over and squeezed Grace's hand and said, "Grace, we would like you to come and stay with us until you can get back on your feet." Jim stood beside her, smiling.

Grace looked at them, and the tears that had been threatening finally fell freely. "I would love that. Thank you," she said, relieved to have such a safe place to go to. It would help her to get some perspective on the world and allow her to be herself again. She needed to find work and discover who *Grace* was, now, after all that had happened. Grace thought she might join the rowing club in Ottawa to make some friends. She would get in touch with her dad and start the process of forgiving him and getting to know his new family. That would help to put some of that hurt behind her. And as she looked back at Cam, Grace knew that he would be a part of that future too. The only thing that worried her was Sebastian. Where *was* he? She had a funny feeling that she had not seen the last of him.

It was Kat's turn. She took her time, then paused, rereading and nodding to herself. She looked over to Jake and then down to the book. "'Could a greater miracle take place than for us to look through each other's eyes just for an instant?'"

Perfect, Grace thought. That was just perfect for them.

Jake smiled his crooked smile and looked down at his guitar sitting on his lap. He gazed up at Kat as she gave him the book with a twinkle in her eye. He took it and opened the book, finding one in an instant. "'When I hear music, I fear no danger. I am invulnerable. I see no foe.

I am related to the earliest times, and to the latest,'" he said with a little flair.

They all chuckled at the appropriateness of the words and the way he had presented them.

Jim stood and reached over to take the book back, then sat down, placing it on the arm of his chair and putting his hand on it with finality. They were done with it. They had learned their lessons. Inspired, Jake began tuning his guitar, and as he prepared to play, Grace looked at the faces sitting around the fire, each lost in their own thoughts. They listened as he played a familiar tune, one of Grace's favorites. The last week had been crazy, life-changing. She realized that although she'd had been responsible for leaving Peterborough and ending up here at Thompson Lake, how the week had played out had not been under her control. Jason dying had not been her fault. Even so, she felt responsible. Leaving him had created a ripple effect that had taken them here. Where it would take her next, only time would tell. She would have to put the fear and guilt behind her and move forward. But, like the song suggested, people have to make difficult decisions in life. Although we are forever changed by some, we must make the best of it and hold on to the good memories. This week was a turning point if ever there was one.

Maybe she would get that tattoo after all.

AFTERWORD

L IFE WITH CHILDREN IS BUSY. WHILE MY HUSBAND AND I were running the kids to their activities and helping them with their school assignments, a big part of me was missing who I used to be.

I missed the carefree times when I could count on hanging out with my friends on a Friday night. I missed being able to go camping on a whim. I reminisced about a time when I was figuring out who I was and what I wanted out of life. Although I didn't want to have to go through all that again, I did realize it was a special time and one which made me who I am today.

I started writing *Northern Escape* in order to capture memories of those days, many of which happened during the five years I lived in Ontario. They were memorable partly because I was there on my own and my friends were my family, and because they were memorable, I wanted to tell my family about some of the adventures I'd had.

As we live, we see things, read things, and hear things and we want to protect our children from them. These, too, were some of the reasons for wanting to write this story. I wanted to capture important messages in my writing— messages such as choosing your partner carefully, staying away from drugs, asking for help when you're feeling down, and not letting anyone treat you poorly.

Northern Escape is fictional. This story did not happen to me; it was an adventure I created as I wrote. The similarities end with the settings and tidbits of things I love and worry about. I hope it brought awareness to certain issues, but most importantly, I simply hope you enjoyed the story.

ACKNOWLEDGMENTS

I have many people I would like to thank.

MY AUNT DIANA was the first person I told that I was going to write a book. We had monthly dates at the theatre, and during our visits, we would discuss how it was going. She made me believe it was worthwhile and shared in the excitement with me. She was the first to review my initial revision.

MY SISTER WENDY has always encouraged me to do more than I thought I was capable of. She reviewed *Northern Escape* in its early stages and was there with words of support to take it to the finish line.

MY SON MATTHEW, who is eleven now, has been my cheerleader ever since I finished my first edit in 2016 when he said "Good job, Mom!" after I'd announced I'd finished fixing up the last chapter. Through the past six months, he has been by my side, sitting on the floor reading a book and making sure I knew he was available to talk through anything that needed discussing. His enthusiasm and belief in me have helped more than he knows.

MY HUSBAND DAN helped me find the courage to tell people about this story back when I was first sharing it with family members. He did again as I worked through my nervousness about telling the world that I was a writer and that I had written a book. He was my anchor and provided the calm encouragement that I could do it and it would turn out all right.

To Jenn, Deb, and Rebecca who read through the first "finished" version of *Northern Escape* and were kind with their feedback. I remember Jenn saying, "It's good, but there needs to be *more*." She was right, and I think there is more now.

This story was written for my daughters, Lauren and Sarah. I wanted to prepare them for the big bad world out there and tell them to be careful. They were always there to quietly listen if I needed to run something by them, especially anything related to social media.

I have been super lucky finding a group of professionals that honestly made the process of self-publishing easy, straightforward, and fun.

They are:

Shayla Raquel: I stumbled across Shayla Raquel's book *The 10 Commandments of Author Branding* in the summer of 2020, and it was exactly what I needed. Through that book and her website, I felt like I had gotten to know her and knew she would tell me what needed to be done clearly and simply, so I approached her to edit my book. She pointed out areas that needed work and gave me the tools to improve them. Shayla, I can't thank you enough. You took this book from a cool story with some awkward parts to one that I am proud to share. As I read through *Northern Escape* today, I see my words, my voice, and that thrills me. I feel you have a real talent and—like that little magic wand used to edit a photograph—you made this book shine!

LISA LANDRIE: The photographs that Lisa took gave me the professional images I required to create a beautiful website and provide a nice headshot for this book, but honestly, I had so much fun with her and she brought out the best in me. These pictures lifted me up and gave me so much confidence at a time when I needed it most.

MONICA HAYNES: Monica created the cover for *Northern Escape* and was a dream to work with. She always got changes back to me earlier than I expected them, often within a couple of hours or even minutes. The process couldn't have gone smoother, and I look forward to working with her again.

MELINDA MARTIN: Melinda is a bundle of energy—personality plus! Her extensive experience and professionalism let me know as soon as I spoke with her that I had nothing to worry about. I knew she would do an amazing job with my interior formatting!

Thank you also to my cousin-in-law **ANDREA** for providing me information on jurisdiction, protocol, and terminology as related to the law enforcement scenes in this book. Her knowledge was extremely helpful. I do want to say, though, that I may have taken creative license in one or two spots and anything that wasn't done *by the book* is completely my fault.

I want to say a special thanks to ALL OF MY FRIENDS who have been supporting me online. Your likes and comments inspire me!

TO MY BFFs—you know who you are—although we haven't had a chance to get together lately, I know you are there if I need you and that means so much.

And, last but not least, to my parents, **BILL AND DOROTHY**. Thank you for always supporting me.

ABOUT THE AUTHOR
Cindy Folk

CINDY FOLK was born and raised in Regina, Saskatchewan, Canada. She attended the University of Regina, majoring in finance. The co-operative education program there took her to work terms in Toronto and Ottawa. After university, she moved to Ottawa, where she competed in rowing and had the opportunity to explore Eastern Canada and the United States. She moved home in 1998 and met and married her husband, Dan. They now have three children. Although her work environment is very structured, Cindy has always had a creative side that was bubbling just below the surface, waiting to be discovered. Writing has allowed that part of her to flourish. *Northern Escape* is her debut novel.

Connect with the Author

cindyfolkauthor.com
Facebook.com/cindyfolkauthor
Twitter.com/cr_folk
Instagram.com/cindyfolkauthor

Book Club Discussion Guide

Visit cindyfolkauthor.com to receive your
Book Club Discussion Guide.

Leave a Review

If you enjoyed *Northern Escape*, will you please consider writing a review on the platform of your choice? Reviews help indie authors find more readers like you.

28494990R00159